C000111089

Could This Be Love

Love Blossoms, Volume 1

CD Giles

Published by CD Giles, 2022.

Table of Contents

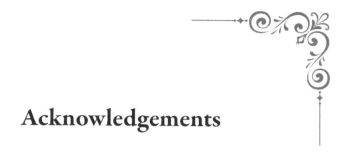

Acknowledgements

I have to start by thanking my hubby. If it wasn't for you showing me that happily ever after does exist, I would have never had the inspiration to write. I love you babe. Thanks for always believing in me and giving me the confidence to believe that my dreams can come true.

To my ray of sunshine, thank you for being in this journey with me. You helped me in more ways than I can count. Love you to the moon and back.

To my family, thank you for your love and dedication throughout the years. I have some strong role models who have helped me navigate this world. You give me strength with your love that fuels me. I love you with all my heart.

My girl tribe – what can I say – you have been my rock throughout the years. I know that I can call at any hour of the day and you'll be there. Thank you for helping me harness my girl power. Love you to pieces.

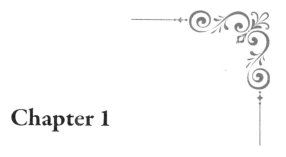

Chapter 1

Gabi

I look down at my smart watch and realize that I should have headed down to the bar on the promenade deck about ten minutes earlier. This is the last time slot before they close for the evening and I really need a drink after the day that I've had, plus I wanted to experience this bar because of its uniqueness. The bar is on hydraulics and rises about six stories for breathtaking views of the evening sky with seating for no more than 20 people. It's a cute setup with bar top tables set for two along the perimeter of the bar and three barstools at the bar. I read on a blog that it's best to go to the bar on the first day if you want to experience it because passengers begin to discover it as time on the ship progresses making it difficult to book.

I'm power walking now trying to make it to my destination. I wish that I hadn't promised my boss that he would have my report by Monday morning. I saw the glimmer in his eyes when I said it because he knows that I would never miss a deadline.

I begin to slow my pace because I can see the bar up ahead and there are only a few patrons mingling. I'm glad because this bar has been on my list since my friend, Samantha, and I booked the cruise.

I walk up to the bar on a mission. I've earned this drink after working eight hours straight...*while on vacation!*

"Hi." I look down at the bartender's name tag, "Mark from Poland." Then I whisper, "Can I have a Sex on the Beach?"

I hear someone chuckle besides me, darn, I guess I didn't actually whisper the embarrassing cocktail name as quietly as I thought. I look to my right and find the sharpest green eyes that I've ever seen. I swear that he's looking right through me, and that light scruff that he has going on is doing things to my lady parts that have lain dormant for far too long.

"Sooooo, Sex on the Beach....is that on your to-do list for this cruise?"

"Oh, my, no...I mean I don't know...I'm going to shut up now." I can't believe he's talking to me. Why the hell am I stuttering? You know why Gabi...this white boy is F-I-N-E. Okay Gabi, play it cool. He can't tell that it's been two years, three months and ten days since your last non-electronically induced orgasm.

Jake

This girl is beyond beautiful. She has light caramel skin with long, light brown straight hair and blond highlights. Her eyes look like they're a hazel green and her body is beyond perfection. She's wearing a sleeveless, turquoise maxi dress that is fitted, showing off her trim waist and toned arms. I'm so checking her out but I'm trying to be cool about it while trying not to take a sneak peek at her breasts.

I go with keeping my eyes above her chest and chuckle because this girl is a riot. I already feel lighter just from being around her and can't stop smiling. "Hi Sex on the Beach, I'm Jake," as I reach over to shake her hand. She doesn't immediately try to take my hand so I add, "This is where you give me your name."

"Yessssss...you're right, that is how it's supposed to work – I'm Gabi." I'm glad that he didn't give his last name. I just met this guy and my dad drilled into me you need to always be smart, cautious.

"I hope that you don't mind me asking, but why are you in this bar alone?"

"I came on this cruise with my best friend. We had everything planned, then she met a guy while we were in line waiting to check in. They hit it off and have been together ever since. How about you?"

"I needed some time to decompress. My friend wanted to go to the nightclub, and I wanted something quieter, so here I am."

I looked down and didn't even realize that I'd finished my drink. Before ordering a drink for myself, my mom raised me to be a gentleman first so I ask, "Gabi, would you like another drink?" She nods 'yes' so I raise my fingers to signal another round from the bartender.

"Any fun facts about you, Jake?"

"Well, I have a twin sister, but I'm the oldest and I never let her forget who's the boss. I've lived in the same town all my life except when I went away for college. You wouldn't know this by looking at me but I've been a Lego geek most of my life. I love *Star Trek* (old, new, TV shows and movies). Now that I'm pretty sure that I've probably scared you away. I need to know - are you a *Star Trek* fan?"

"Sorry Jake, I have never watched Star Trek, but I have heard of it."

"Well, you're in luck! I happened to notice that they'll be showing a *Star Trek* movie under the stars on Wednesday. Maybe we can go – you really need to see at least one movie before making any snap judgment – let me be your *Star Trek* guide."

Gabi

Jake gives me a charming smile...it's a sweet, possibly bashful and maybe a little naughty, I'm not sure. I'm so off my game right now it's not even funny. I bet he's gotten away with a lot with just that look. A mother wouldn't be able to punish him.

"OK, Jake, I'll make you a deal. We both know that this ship is massive. If our paths cross again on the cruise, I'll go to see the *Star Trek* movie with you on Wednesday."

Just then the bar starts descending slowly. I guess our little chat is over. Once we're back on solid ground, I try to settle up my tab, but Jake won't hear of it. He says, "Let me. You have been just what I needed. It's the least I can do."

"Thanks, Jake. I'll see you around."

Jake

I'm smiling ear to ear as Gabi walks off. Before she leaves, I lightly grab her arm and slide down to grab her hand. When I do, I feel a spark. What the hell, must be my imagination. Before I can overthink it, I blurt out, "Gabi, what do you say about grabbing breakfast in the morning?"

"I'm not sure, even though my girlfriend abandoned me today, we planned an excursion to hang out on the beach tomorrow."

"I understand. My best friend, Travis, and I signed up for a day on the water. We have reserved jet skis. How about dinner?" I can't let her just walk away and leave our next meeting up to chance. This ship has over five thousand passengers. My heart is beating like I've ran a marathon, but I push through. I have this overwhelming sense that it's very important that I see Gabi again. "Can I have your room number so I can call you?"

I wince internally as I say it. Gabi is quiet...I can only imagine what she's thinking. I've drilled into my own sister's head "never let a guy know where you live or work until you're absolutely sure about him and even then, check again." It's never paranoid to be cautious when giving personal details to the opposite sex, especially those that you've just met. But I know this for sure, not even if there was a gun held to my head...nothing could keep me from asking for her room number.

"Jake, how about you give me your room number? Do you have a set time for dinner?"

"No, I signed up for the flexible dining option so I could pick my dining time each evening."

"Me too, want to meet on level 8 at seven?"

COULD THIS BE LOVE

"Yes, I'll even make the reservation so we don't have to wait in the long line. I'm in room 14256. Have a good night, Gabi. See you tomorrow night."

Chapter 2

G abi
   Three days ago when my world shifted

"Dr. Robinson, is there something that you need to discuss with me? The nurse asked that I not check out until you had an opportunity to talk to me."

"Gabi, it's probably nothing but I'd like to be sure. I thought that I heard something with the stethoscope and would feel better if we do further tests to understand if there is actually anything going on or not. I'm going to order an echocardiogram and a few other tests."

"Do I need to get the tests immediately, like, today?" I'm trying not to panic, but I can tell that my anxiety is rising.

"I know that you're leaving for your vacation tomorrow. If I thought that we needed to get these done today before you leave, I would say so. You can get the test at your earliest convenience. Once scheduled, make an appointment with me for a follow-up. We'll go over the results at that time."

"Sounds good."

I'm driving home after the appointment a little shell shocked. Dr. Robinson has been my doctor for almost five years now. I trust her and know that she would have made an emergency appointment if she felt it was necessary. This makes me feel a little better but I am worried nonetheless.

My best friend since third grade, Samantha, and I are headed to Miami tomorrow morning to spend a day hanging out before our week-long Eastern Caribbean cruise. Sam has wanted me to have more work/life balance, but my work is my life. I've never taken her seriously (*why would I...I'm only twenty-eight and understand that I need to put in the extra time now to establish my career*) ...maybe I should try to live more in the moment...the cruise would be a great start. Thank goodness that she's spending a night tonight. We didn't want to leave two cars at the airport.

SAM WALKS IN WITH A sushi from our favorite restaurant. I love this girl. She's the sister that I never had.

After sushi and another glass of moscato, I tell Sam about my conversation with the doctor. "I would be lying if I told you that I'm not a little worried. What if there is something going on?"

"Let's not buy worry for now. We'll cross this bridge together whatever it is. You know that I'm with you through thick and thin."

"Love you sis. I don't know what I'd do without you."

"We'll you're never going to have to find out...I want you to hear me out." I give her the side eye. "No, side eye either. I want you to look at this as a blessing in disguise. I've been telling you for a while now that you need to start taking it easy and live in the moment. We're officially on vacation starting tomorrow. If you meet a guy on this cruise, I want you to at least not blow him off. If you're really adventurous, I'd say go out to dinner with him."

"You of all people know me. Me, striking up a conversation with some random guy and agreeing to go out on a date, all seems pretty unbelievable."

Present Day

"How was your date?" I say as I look at Samantha. I can't even be mad at her. She's had a horrendous year and needs this vacation as much as I do.

"It was so much fun. Derek is both parts hilarious and serious, plus hella smart. Our day yesterday flew by. He loves art, so we asked Guest Services for the guide book that shows where the art is throughout the ship. It was amazing. I never would have thought there would be so much art to see on a cruise ship. We had lunch, hung by the pool after taking the tour, then grabbed dinner. Gab, I'm sorry that I abandoned you yesterday. I know that is not what we planned."

"Sam, you know I'm not mad. I'm glad you had a good time. Are you going to see him again?"

"Gurll, you know it. We're getting together for dinner then going to one of the nightclubs. They have salsa dancing lessons before the club opens. We've both never done it so we're going to give it a try. How about you? You're not planning to work, are you? Don't think that I didn't notice that you purchased the Internet package. I thought that you were planning to unplug."

"I promise I'll limit myself to only checking my email once no more than twice."

She gives me the look – she knows that I'm full of it and that I worked for eight hours yesterday in our room. What can I say, at least I worked from the deck and had the view from the balcony of the ocean as my window.

We settle into enjoying the beach. I'm always amazed that we never run out of things to talk about but are happy to just be and let the waves be the backdrop. I don't know why I don't tell her about Jake. I want to, but what if he doesn't show up for dinner? What if it was just one moment, and he decided to move on, or that he doesn't date Black girls? What am I saying, I've never dated a White guy and this is not a date, it's just dinner. But...it kind of feels like a date.

"Wish we could find a way to bring this beach back with us to Austin. This is the perfect day. Did you remember to put on your sunscreen? You know how you burn so easily."

"Yes, mom –I mean Sam – I lathered up. Did I tell you that I found this new sunscreen for sensitive skin? That should help me avoid getting sunburned on my face."

I decide to change the subject because once Sam gets going with her mothering vibe, she'll never stop. I notice that the DJ has switched to reggae.

"Gurll – this is the jam. I can't believe that we're finally here, and the music is off the chain. I'm ready for a Bahama mama though – where did the waitress go?"

Once our drinks arrive, I take a huge sip and sigh. "Now this is what I needed. Let's get this party started right!" I turn to look at Sam with a huge grin on my face. "Do you remember our senior trip?"

"You know that I do. You could always depend on Byron to sneak in alcohol. Our chaperones were either clueless or they didn't care. I never danced or laughed so much. We really turned up our senior year. They'll never forget the class of '09. We were the best class ever."

I HAD TO COME BACK to the room early so I could take a nap then start getting ready for dinner. I don't have a clue what to wear but I do know that I need to wash, blow dry, and flat iron my hair.

I'm finally ready with fifteen minutes to spare. I take one more look in the full-length mirror before heading out. I smile – I look pretty good. But I had to channel my inner Beyoncé to stop a panic attack. Thank God for Bey – I chose a flowy, fuchsia sundress in her honor with strappy sandals. Now, let's go rock Jake's world.

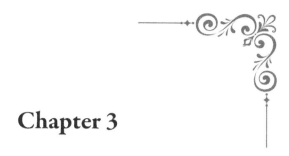

Chapter 3

Jake

I'm damn near pacing but trying to look cool – where is she – I hope she's not bailing on me – I kept checking my room phone expecting her to cancel on me – I keep looking down at my watch – well, damn, it's not even seven o'clock yet – I guess I was anxious to get here – I catch a whiff of a beautiful floral scent and turn slowly to find Gabi. My god, she's gorgeous and way out of my league. She can't be more than five foot five inches in those strappy sandals which is the perfect height for me. I can tell that she's been out in the sun today. She's got a perfect golden glow to her skin. She's wearing her hair down again. I love how it flows when she walks. Don't fuck this up Jake. Play it cool, man. Get it together.

"Gabi, you look gorgeous. How was your official first full day of the cruise?" I bend and give her a quick peck on the cheek then begin to lead her to the front of the line. "We can actually go to the left side. They should be calling us any minute since we have reservations."

My name is called. The maître d hands us over to the waiter who takes us to our seat. I have my hand on the small of Gabi's back because I need an excuse to touch her. Before the waiter can pull out Gabi's seat, I intervene and damn near tackle the poor guy. I see Gabi hide her smile. I guess that I wasn't as smooth as I thought I was.

Gabi

I'm still quietly laughing when Jake takes his seat. His last name sounds familiar but I'm not sure where I've heard Jake McAdams before.

Jake is looking even more handsome tonight than he did yesterday. I can now tell that he has to be at least six foot two. The suit he's wearing looks designer. It hangs off his body like it was made for him, which I'm pretty sure it was.

I look up to realize that Jake has been talking to me but I was totally zoned out. "I'm sorry, can you repeat that again?"

"I was just asking if you'd like wine or a mixed drink with your dinner."

"I would love some wine. How about you pick it? I'm trying to expand my palette."

"Sure, what do you like – dry, sweet, fruity?"

"I don't know. I'm just starting to try wines. Can you pick something middle of the road since I'm just north of a novice?"

"Nothing about you screams novice, but I know just the one that I'll order for us."

I'm blushing now and there's not anything that I can do about it. He is so attentive and different from anybody that I've dated before, regardless of race. I love how he makes me feel like I'm the only woman in the room. I have his full attention, but not in a creepy way. He's leaning forward with a welcoming smile – I can so get used to this.

We place our orders, and once the waiter leaves, I have an opportunity to appreciate where we're seated. Jake was able to snag a table with an ocean view. It's perfect and very romantic. I wonder how he made this happen. These tables are prime real estate. I want to know his secret. Who am I kidding? I want to know more than this secret. Patience – as my grandmother used to say, good things come to those who wait. The butterflies that I feel lets me know that I'm excited about tonight.

The sommelier comes to our table with the bottle of wine that Jake ordered. He shows Jake the bottle then opens it and pours a small amount in Jake's glass. Jake does exactly like I've seen on TV – he takes a small sip, lets the wine rest on his tongue, slight swish, then swallow. I'm mesmerized. Who knew watching someone drink wine could be so sexy? He gives a slight nod, then the sommelier fills my glass first then Jake's.

Jake raises his glass. "To new beginnings."

"To new beginnings." I take my first sip. I don't know what I was expecting, but this wine is smooth and flavorful. "This is very good. I definitely approve. You have me wondering what else you have in store for the evening."

"I booked two options and will be happy to do either. You'll be able to decide which one we do this evening. You're not going to believe this when I say that I'm normally not one who likes to plan surprises for someone, but with you I find that I'm very motivated."

Now, here I go blushing again – this man is something else and I'm liking every minute of it. "Tell me more about yourself Jake."

"As I mentioned, I'm a twin. My sister is Jacqueline but we call her Jacqi (pronounced Jackie). I'm embarrassed to say that my parents spoiled us and may have gone a little over board when we were growing up."

"I'm an only child and understand what it means to be spoiled. Now, you've got me intrigued, what's your favorite memory?"

Jake smiles for a moment before starting, "For our fourth birthday, my parents had a carnival themed party with pony rides, carnival rides, funnel cakes, corn dogs – everything. I had a blast. I even won a stuffed animal knocking down all the milk cans."

Jake hasn't mentioned that he comes from a wealthy family, but hearing this story leads me to believe that he is. I may be wrong here but I don't think you normally see interracial dating in the upper class of society. I know that this isn't applicable to us since we won't see each other after the cruise, but definitely makes me wonder.

"I love this story, Jake. I bet after that party all the kids wanted to be invited each year." Jake turns bright red. I'm laughing now "No, Jake, really…am I right?"

"Yeah, you're right. Every year the invite list would get larger and larger. My mom finally put her foot down with the number of kids that we could invite."

Jake

I must be doing okay. Gabi has been laughing throughout dinner and hasn't mentioned that she's ready to end our date.

I clear my throat nervously. "I wasn't sure what you'd like to do after dinner. How would you like to see *Chicago,* the musical or the diving show?"

"Jake, I'd love to go see *Chicago.* I've always wanted to see it but for one reason or another, I could never make it work."

"Well, it's your lucky day. I booked the 9:00 show in case you'd like to go. I booked the diving show as well. The good news is our reservations for the diving show are automatically cancelled fifteen minutes before showtime if we're a no show. Now, we have a few routes that we can take to get there. Would you prefer to stay inside or walk outside?"

"I'd normally vote for fresh air, but with the wind picking up, I'm afraid what my hair will look like by the time that we get to the show."

"Understand, no further explanation required." I grab her hand because I can't help myself. Every time that I touch her, it feels so right. I wonder if she feels this connection. I've never felt this before.

We have plenty of time, so I decide to walk us through the indoor park. I couldn't ask for a better setting – there's a four-person string quartet led by a singer who is singing low, weaving a romantic ambience. I find a private alcove where we can listen to the music.

"Now, Jake, if I didn't know better…."

I don't give her time to finish her sentence. I turn her, cradle her neck and weave my fingers into her hair while leaning down to finally get the kiss that I've been dreaming about. I slowly kiss her lips and finally lightly lick her lips. I'm trying my damnedest to go slow and not scare her away. She opens for me, and I don't waste a minute. I savor her like I savored the first taste of the wine. She tastes like a mixture of the wine and chocolate lava cake that she had at dinner. I want to keep going but I'm about to embarrass myself if I'm not careful. I step away so she won't feel the effect that she has on me. The last thing that I want is for her to think that I only want one thing from her...I want it all but I can't tell her my intentions yet. She'll think that I've lost my mind and can't very well want to spend the rest of my life with someone that I only met twenty-four hours ago.

I bend my forehead down to hers, close my eyes and just breath in her scent. I'm quickly becoming addicted to her scent. She smells like roses and vanilla. It's uniquely Gabi, no one else could smell like her. I'm glad to see Gabi is breathing as hard as I am. I'd hate for this to be one-sided.

"I'm sorry, I didn't bring you over here to devour you."

She gives me that look and lifts her eyebrow – both parts sassy and saucy. She's busting my balls and I don't even care.

"I was actually starting to worry that I wasn't kiss worthy. You've assuaged my worries. Can I ask you something?"

"Yes, of course anything"

"Would you do that again?"

I swear one second doesn't even pass. I'm delving right in but this time I've pulled her all the way to me. She feels my arousal and makes a sound that lets me know she's happy to discover this new development. I continue to kiss her with everything that I've got. Our tongues are dueling then I hold onto her tongue and begin rhythmically sucking it. I want her to know that I'm very much into her. Even though she doesn't know that she's the only one for me. She'll figure it out soon enough.

I finally pull away. I'm glad to see the arousal in her eyes. If I wanted this to be just a cruise fling, I'd say forget the play, but that's not the plan.

"Let's sit for a while before heading to the musical. I want to just hold you while we enjoy the music."

Gabi

I was sure after feeling Jake's arousal that we'd be on our way to one of our rooms. I'm a surprised and a little disappointed, but I go ahead and sit on the bench with Jake.

After a few minutes, I find myself leaning on his shoulder and enjoying the music. Wow, this is really nice. I love that Jake doesn't feel the need to fill the silence. The song changes and it's one of my favorites. Jake hears me humming.

"Gabi, would you like to dance?"

"Here, now?"

"Yes, here and now."

He slowly stands and holds out his hand. I grab his hand and find myself in his strong arms. I'm shocked that it's not awkward. I normally don't know where to put my hands. I place my left hand in his and lay my head on his shoulder as he begins to sway. The music is transcending. This is magical, and I don't want the night to end. If he asks me to spend the night, should I? I just met him. I don't want him to get the wrong idea about me. I'm not that type of girl. I'm conservative to a fault. My bad side says girl, you only live once and this guy is HOT. My bad side is winning out. I'm into Jake. I finally make up my mind. I want to see where tonight takes us.

The song has ended but Jake continues to sway. He's weaving a spell like nobody's business. He finally stops. I look up to find Jake looking at me as if he's seeing something new.

"What?"

"Nothing – I'm finding that I love just holding you...it's my new favorite thing."

"You won't get any complaints from me. I love being in your arms."

"As much as I'd like to stay here, we've got to get moving to get seated for the show."

Jake

I can tell that Gabi is impressed with our seats. I was able to secure box seats.

"What do you think?"

"Jake, these seats are amazing. You keep surprising me. I better be careful. A girl could get used to this."

"I haven't even gotten started, but I'm glad that you like it. Do you want anything?"

"I'd like a half glass of wine so I'm not mixing my alcohol. My friends call me a lightweight."

"Well, don't be embarrassed. I think that's cute."

The waiter takes our order. When he returns, he shares that there is a private bathroom available for our use (well us and the other three couples).

The musical starts after the waiter has brought our drinks.

I can tell that Gabi is loving the musical. She leans forward and at times appears to hold her breath as she's watching the scene unfold. I've seen this musical several times. My dad hates going to see Broadway musicals so I would often be my mom's date. I'm not bored though. I could sit here and watch Gabi all night.

Beautiful doesn't even begin to describe her. I swear that I've never seen eyes like hers. At times they appear to be hazel and other times, a mesmerizing green.

I realize that Gabi is staring at me. I should be embarrassed about getting caught admiring her, but I'm not. The first two acts have ended and the theater lights are on signaling intermission.

I use this opportunity to pull Gabi close against my side.

"How are you liking it so far?"

"The jailhouse scene was my favorite, and to think that the lawyer is taking advantage of the defendant to make sure his name stays in the newspaper – for shame."

"Yeah, this is one of my mom and sister's favorite. It's a must see when it's scheduled to be in town." I lean forward because I want an excuse to pull her even closer and whisper in her ear. "Do you need anything?"

"No, I think I'm good for now."

I can't let this opportunity pass without flirting a little. "Are you sure there's not anything that you want?"

Gabi

I can't with this man. I'm not used to all this flirting. I've lost count of the number of times that he's made me blush. You'd think that I was sixteen and on my very first date.

This musical is off the chain. I really need to make more time once I'm back home to enjoy things like this. I'm at the point where I'm making a good living but I work all the time so I'm not spending it.

The best part is being here with Jake. I want to ask how he was able to secure the best seats in the theatre. He definitely appears to have the hookup, but this is one of the rare times where I'm enjoying the surprise.

Jake has been holding me close since intermission started. Once the musical's second half began, I was surprised that he didn't release his hold. This is becoming one of my favorite places.

Jake

The musical is almost over. It will be close to midnight once the musical ends. I'm open to continuing the date but I don't want to monopolize all of her time.

Once the lights are back up, I ask "Well, did it meet your expectations?"

"Yes, I didn't see the ending coming. It kept me practically on the edge of my seat by the end."

"I could tell. What would you like to do next?"

"I hate to be a Debbie Downer but I'm actually pretty tired. Would it be okay if we call it a night?"

"Yes, absolutely. Let me at least walk you back to your room."

"Thanks, Jake. I appreciate it."

"What do you have planned tomorrow?"

"My roommate has made other plans again so I really wasn't sure."

"What's your excursion?"

"It was a Vespas scooter tour of the island with lunch at a beachside restaurant before heading back to the ship. I'd rather not do the excursion alone."

"If you're not sick of me, I'd love to hang out. I've never ridden a Vespa – it actually sounds fun and the weather is supposed to be ideal tomorrow."

"This was one of the excursions that I'd starred on the planner for this cruise."

"Great, now you don't have to cancel. What time do I need to pick you up?"

"Don't hate me, but we have to be down by 9:30."

"That works for me. Do you want to grab breakfast before we head out?"

"Breakfast sounds heavenly. How about 8:30? I found this cool grill by the pool that makes made-to-order omelets."

Gabi

We left the theatre and have arrived to the elevators.

"Gabi, which floor should I push?"

"14"

"Really? That's the same floor as mine."

"Yeah, I realized we were on the same floor when you gave me your room number." I start laughing.

Jake is shaking his head, but I can tell he's having as much fun as I am.

We make it to my door much faster than I'm ready for. I don't want this date to end yet.

I turn to say goodnight. "Jake, I had a great night."

Before I know it, Jake has turned me completely around and bends to kiss me. This kiss is off the charts. I place my fingers in Jake's hair. His hair feels as nice as I thought it would. It's thick and extremely soft. I love how it feels in my hands. I need to keep up. Jake has now changed the kiss. It's deeper, slower, and more sensual.

When the kiss ends, we're both breathing like we ran five miles. I can't think straight when he's this close.

"You, Jake, are more than I expected."

Jake

"Gabi, I was thinking the same thing. You've blown me away. I'll see you in the morning."

"I had a wonderful time tonight."

"I did too. Dream of me."

I start to walk away then turn back to see her checking me out. I wink and head to my room as fast as I can. I'm hard as a rock. I hope Travis hasn't made it back. This is embarrassing enough.

I KNOCK ON GABI'S DOOR at 8:30 on the dot. She opens it immediately and my breath is taken away. She stands before me in the cutest blue jean shorts and yellow halter top that I've seen. Her hair is curly in a high ponytail. "Good morning gorgeous. Ready to get our day started? Oh crap, I may be speaking way too loud for your friend."

"No, she left early this morning with the guy that she met. They're going on a six-hour catamaran and snorkeling tour."

"Sounds like fun – is this something that is on your list for the week?"

"No not me – I'd rather watch the water from the beach than get in the water. Did you see Jaws?" (Jake nods his head 'yes'). "Well, I did too and it scared the shit out of me."

I bark out a laugh from my gut. She cracks me up. I can't remember the last time that I've laughed as much as I have since I've met her.

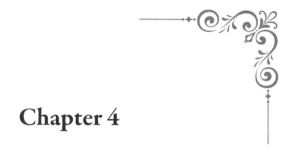

Chapter 4

G abi

Our Vespas tour guide has been leading us on a sightseeing tour through St. Maarten. We have microphones in our helmets so we can hear the historical facts of the island as we head to our destination. Hearing that the island changed hands multiple times between the Dutch, French, and Spaniards, now explains why the island is split and has two different spelling variations for the name.

I picked this tour for the outdoor beachfront restaurant that serves the best codfish fritters on the island. Once we arrive to the restaurant, I look around and sigh contentedly. "Isn't this the perfect place, Jake? If you would have asked me which island is your favorite, I would have answered, hands down, Aruba. Now, I love this one just as much"

"What do you like about it?" Jake looks at me as if he really cares about my answer.

"It has its own rhythm. With the sapphire blue water and island breeze from the ocean, it's calming and has a 'finding my center' vibe to it. The live reggae band definitely adds to the ambiance. What about you? How does this location measure up to places where you have been?"

He looks at me intently. "This is on the top of my list for many reasons. The view from my vantage point is magnificent."

He's not talking about the island. He's talking about me. Is this guy for real, or is he just trying to get me into bed? I've never been good at reading guys. I've dated off and on, plus had one serious guy, Richard.

In retrospect, I now realize that the relationship with him lasted as long as it did because we were comfortable with each other. There was no spark, no common interests. I wasted over a year with that guy before I realized that I needed to cut him loose.

Instead of responding to Jake's comment, I look down at my rum punch. I'm quiet for a while then say the first thing that pops into my head. "I'm surprised that you haven't asked me what I am."

"What do you mean – what you are? Are you talking about whether you're of the female gender?"

"No, what's my racial makeup?"

"Do you get that question a lot?"

"You wouldn't believe how often I get that question. If I had a dollar for every time someone asked me, I could retire by now."

"I would never ask you that Gabi. First of all, I think that it's a racist and offensive thing to ask someone. I don't expect you to ask where I come from. Second of all, I'm happy to just be in your presence and that you have decided to spend your time with me. I don't get the impression that you let just anyone in."

He nailed it – I'm equal parts shocked and surprised. Shocked because I was prepared to talk about my lineage (I've said it so many times that it's like an elevator speech for me) and surprised because he appears to know me better than some people who have known me practically my entire life. He's been so open with me. I find myself wanting to know more about him and decide in this moment that I will be more open. I originally thought that I should not share my last name but I've changed my mind. It's a woman's prerogative after all. "What do you do when you're not on vacation having lunch on the beach?" I'm smiling and leaning in.

"I'm an architect."

"What do you like most about being an architect?"

"I love having the opportunity to design something that will be around even after I'm long gone. The best part is traveling to the site and meeting the client to hear their vision. What do you do when you're not on vacation having lunch on the beach?"

I love that he kicks the same question back to me. "I'm an analyst for a venture capitalist firm. I research untapped companies, assess their value, and recommend percentage ownership that includes cash infusion." I usually hide this side of myself because I've had guys who were intimidated by my career.

Jake

I wonder if Gabi was going to say something else at first. I could tell that she had something on her mind then I noticed a shift. I'll be here when she's ready to talk no matter what it is.

I go along for now. "I'm impressed." I love how her eyes shine when she talks. I'm mesmerized. "I find what you do fascinating. How did you get into the field?"

"After graduation, I was working in a consulting firm doing mergers and acquisitions. I found that I liked seeing young companies mature and integrate into larger ones which statistically meant that the company will survive. It's sad once you become aware that most new start-ups don't make it. I became more and more interested in helping start-up companies that were strapped for cash and needed an angel investor to have a chance to grow so I switched to VC."

WE FINISH OUR LUNCH and start heading back to the ship. Our guide is leading the way and I'm bringing up the rear. I want to keep Gabi in my sights to make sure that she's safe and doesn't run into issues with her scooter. This girl has quickly gotten into my system and is becoming very important to me. She brings out a protective side in me that up until this point had only been reserved for my mom and sister. Now, I need to figure out how to make her mine forever. I'm losing the battle to take it slow. I don't want to scare her off. Remember to play it cool, Jake – you've always been a planner – just take your time (hopefully if I keep telling myself this, I'll slow down).

Wow. We made it to the ship faster than I thought. I stop, hop off my scooter and jog over to Gabi so I can help her. "I noticed a few vendors over there. Would you like to go check them out?"

"You really don't mind shopping? I'm shocked."

"No, not at all – remember I have a mom and sister who quickly learned one of my assets is holding bags of all sizes."

I take her hand, and we stroll to the booths.

She stops to look at a few swimsuit coverups. She is trying to decide between a sheer fuchsia, purple, or teal. I have some favorites that I know would look phenomenal on her.

"Gabi, just my two cents, all of them will look great on you but I'd go with either the purple or teal ones."

"Yeah, I'm leaning towards the purple one too. It will go nicely with one of the swimsuits that I bought for the trip."

If there is a god in heaven, I'll have an opportunity to see Gabi in that swimsuit before this trip is over.

After haggling with the merchant, she makes her purchase. I can tell that she's very pleased with her negotiating skills. She was able to save almost twenty dollars. I'd say she did very good. I'm impressed as well. "Do you mind if we pop into that jewelry store? I'd like to see if I can find something for my mom and sister."

"Not at all."

We browse. Before long, I notice that Gabi is lingering over a beautiful necklace. She tries it on. It looks amazing against her skin. She asks for the price, then shakes her head no. I make a mental note to come back after dropping her back on the ship. I know that if I offer to buy it for her now, she'll refuse.

I find something that I know is going to make my sister scream with delight. I can already imagine her reaction. We wander around a little bit more when I notice that Gabi is yawning. "Would you like to head back?"

"I'm sorry – I'm trying to hang in there but I'm exhausted from being out in the heat."

WE'VE MADE IT BACK to her room in record time. "I don't want to monopolize all of your time but I'd love to take you to dinner and a show tonight."

She looks at me as if surprised. "Isn't tonight the formal night?"

"Yes, it is – were you planning to stay in your room and just order room service?"

"Actually, I hadn't figured out what I was doing tonight yet. Are you sure that you're not sick of me by now?"

"Gabi, I'd spend all day and night for the rest of the cruise if I thought you'd be open to this. Before you go down the wrong path, I'd want to spend a night with you even if we were just looking at the stars all night."

Gabi

This man keeps saying things like this. He can't be for real..can he? He's definitely a smooth talker. Gabi, eyes wide open, girlfriend. Eyes wide open.

"Jake, dinner and a show works for me.

Chapter 5

Gabi

Okay Gabi girl, what are we wearing and what are we doing with this hair? I snap my fingers. I got it. I've brought a white lace bustier that has a matching garter and thong. The silk stockings are the perfect addition. More importantly, I feel sexy, confident and empowered. I didn't buy these with Jake in mind but I sure am glad that I did...this is going to make his jaw drop.

I'm ready with five minutes to spare. I'm checking my makeup and went to grab my clutch when there's a knock on the door. After confirming that it's Jake, I open it. Talk about jaw-dropping, it's my jaw that hits the floor. He decided to wear a tux with a tuxedo shirt but kept the top few buttons open. He looks like he belongs on the cover of a magazine.

Jake

My heartbeat immediately starts racing just seeing her stand here in front of me. She decided to wear her hair loose and wavy. I'm speechless. Her dress is sexy and classy at the same time. She's wearing a silver and baby blue off the shoulder gown. I'm the luckiest bastard on this ship.

"Hi, beautiful. How was your nap?"

"Good, I slept like a baby. Let me just grab my clutch."

I CHOSE THE STEAKHOUSE tonight for our date. I'm impressed with the décor. The mahogany wood finish for the tables and walls is accented with rich earth tones throughout on the chairs and carpet. The fixtures have a brushed brass finishing illuminating a subdued lighting. Reminds me of Houston's, a restaurant back home.

We listen to the waiter talk about the specials for tonight. I was able to book a booth that allows for privacy. The booth has a curved high back that allows us to sit and face the wall without having to see the other patrons. I help Gabi slide into the booth and slide in next to her.

We place our orders, and now I finally have her all to myself.

I lean down but pause, realizing that she's wearing something glossy on her lips that I'll mess up if I go in for the kiss that I want so badly.

Gabi whispers, "Jake?"

I love how my name sounds when she says it all soft and slightly out of breath. "Yes, sweetheart?"

"Are you planning to do what I think you going to do?"

"Only if you won't be mad because I may mess up your lipstick."

"Go for it."

I love the slight blush that comes over her. She doesn't have to tell me twice.

I lean the rest of the way and place a soft kiss on her lips. She doesn't pull back so I go back for a deeper kiss, let my tongue come out to play while inviting her to join me. When she does, I go in pulling her closer into my side. Her taste is better than the best wine that I've ever had. I spend a little more time, then finally pull back. "Thank you."

"My pleasure."

I lean back against the back of the booth and let my heartbeat slow down a bit. "What were we talking about? Oh, yes." I lean toward her and take her hand. "You'd mentioned that the St. Claire's are a big family and your parents are both statisticians. How was it growing up with parents' who had prestigious careers?"

"Growing up, I thought that my parents were like every other kids' parents. It wasn't until I left for college that I realized it wasn't normal to have a godparent who'd been awarded a Nobel peace prize. Uncle Ted is great and was the one to encourage me to use my natural gifts with numbers to do something different than my parents. Honestly, I fought it for a long time. I wanted my own identity. Does that make sense?"

"It makes total sense and I get it, no additional explanation required. Where did you go to college? My guess is probably one of the Ivy League schools."

"Very perceptive – I went to Harvard for my undergrad and masters."

"Wow! I must say that I'm in awe. You continue to amaze me. I get the impression that you hide this little-known fact. Why is that?"

Gabi

This man is truly dialed in to me. He seems like he really wants to get to know me. I've never had anyone want to get to know the real me. Usually, guys see the outer appearance and don't take the time to find out if there's anything more there.

"Well, from my experience, the male species is intimidated by females who have an established career, are a high-income earner, and can put more than ten words together. I've found that it's best to not even mention it to avoid any uneasiness on their part."

"Baby, there's nothing about you that I don't find absolutely sexy and yes, I mean your brain and intelligence. There isn't anything that we haven't been able to talk about. Now I understand why – I'm now picturing you at your parents' parties with the best of the best in their field."

How the hell does he know this? My life growing up was surrounded around the intellectual set. My mom made a point of signing me up for soccer, tennis, and dance. This gave me an opportunity to be around kids my own age. Thank god for my mom. If she hadn't done that, I'm pretty sure that I would have been a socially awkward, nerdy kid.

Plus, I love the way that he calls me baby and sweetheart. I'll need time later to digest all the signals that he's sending my way. Every time that he uses a term of endearment, I find myself melting inside and have butterflies (in a good way) on overdrive.

"I bet you were adorable growing up. I can't wait to meet your parents so your mom can show me your baby pictures."

"You're just saying that hoping that you're going to get to second or third base. I'm not a sure bet. You're going to have to work for it, Mr. McAdams."

"I'm counting on it. Don't you worry about me. You can't scare me away easily. I'm all in and more than happy to treat you the way that you deserve to be treated with no strings attached."

Our conversation has been going so well. I'm already on my second glass of wine and half way through my meal. We are both quiet while we listen to the piano playing in the background. "Jake, I meant to tell you earlier that this restaurant is very nice. I appreciate you bringing me here."

WE GET ON THE ELEVATOR. Jake will not tell me where we're going, just that it's a surprise. There is only one couple on the elevator. They're younger...if I had to guess, they appear to be in their early twenties. We end up stopping on the next floor where more couples pile into the elevator. Jake gently pulls me in front of him and wraps his left arm around me so he's blocking anyone from bumping into me. I try to think back to other dates and what they would have done in this exact situation. Hands down, I can't think of one date who would have done this. With Jake, I feel protected and safe when I'm in his arms. A girl could really get used to this.

Jake has his arm draped around me as we walk into the jazz club. The décor is a deep purple with silver metallic contrasts. Crystal chandeliers hang throughout the club giving it a romantic, old jazz club feel. If I didn't know that we were on a cruise ship in the middle of the Caribbean Sea, I'd swear that we were in Manhattan off Fifth Avenue. I finally hear the jazz singer belting out an old standard. Her voice is amazing. She reminds me of Natalie Cole when she released a jazz album later in her career. I immediately gasp and look at him. He winks.

We are led by the hostess to a private section in the corner that has a cushy loveseat and two wingback chairs. It has a table in the middle and great view of the stage. There's a chilled bottle of wine and couple of long-stemmed red roses on the table. As we sit down, I look around and notice that no other tables have roses on them.

When I look back, confused, Jake chimes in, "I requested these for you. I just couldn't resist."

I'm not even going to fight it anymore. I reach up and pull his head down for a light kiss. I should have known that wouldn't be enough. Jake kisses me long and hard – taking his time, but still being appropriate – aware of our surroundings.

After the song has finished, the waiter arrives to open the bottle of wine. Jake never ceases to amaze me. The wine is the one that he knows that I've grown to really like. We sip our wine, enjoying the music, and each other's company. I'm not sure how much time has passed. Jake leans over and asks, "Would you like to dance?"

He puts his hand on the middle of my back, escorting me to the dance floor. His hand is a little lower than casual – if I didn't know better, I'd say that he's sending the signal for any man in the room that I'm his. This sends a shiver up my back in a good way.

As soon as he pulls me into his arms, the singer starts to sing "At Last." We move together like we've been dancing together forever. He sets the perfect tempo – it feels sensual. More importantly, I feel cherished.

Jake

I can tell Gabi is enjoying herself. Having her in my arms feels so right. I have never been one to believe in love at first sight. With Gabi, I'm becoming a believer. Our chemistry is off the charts. Nothing has come close to this, and I was engaged at one time. I now know that I dodged a bullet. To not be able to hold Gabi, hear her laugh, the way she rambles when she gets nervous – I find everything about her absolutely adorable.

After three songs have played, I lean down. "Do you want to go back to our table?"

"Yes, how did you know?"

"As time has passed, you were putting more and more of your weight on me. Don't get me wrong, I'm not complaining, but it just hit me that you've been wearing high heels for a long time now. Let's get you off your feet."

"Bless you, I literally couldn't stand it anymore. I brought some flats with me. Fair warning, our height difference is going to be very obvious whenever we finally walk out of here."

"Well, I'm not worried about that – we make a beautiful couple in my opinion." I wonder if she believes me. "While we enjoy the music, would you like another glass of wine?"

"I'd love one."

After staying for another hour, I lead Gabi to the bank of elevators. I can't believe it – when the elevator arrives, it's empty. We step inside; move to my newfound favorite spot in the back left corner. After turning around and placing Gabi so her back is to my front. I look up to see her looking at us in the mirror. She's right that my six foot two inches to her five foot two inches is obvious but like I said, we make a handsome couple. She's the reason. She's beyond beautiful and has a nice healthy blush. She's lit from the inside, and I feel like I may have a little something to do with it.

"What do you think about coming to my room? You don't have to spend the night if you don't want to stay. You hold all of the cards. I'll take you back to your room any time that you'd like to go. What do you say?" I am damn near begging.

Finally, she puts me out of my misery. She holds my gaze in the mirror and smiles in a way that takes my breath away...and says 'yes'.

To my amazement, we arrive to our floor with no stops. This never happens on a ship this size. I count my blessings and take her straight to my suite.

She looks around. "Wow, we have a suite, too, but yours is amazing. I'll need to book early enough so I can get this one next time."

"I love it. It has an amazing balcony and comes with personal butler. With tomorrow being a sailing day, we can have lunch out on the balcony if you'd like to hangout. It should be a perfect day to be outside, not too hot or humid."

"Jake, I'd love to swing by for lunch."

"Can I get you anything to drink? We have water if you're thirsty."

"No, I'd rather just spend some alone time with you."

I'm not sure if my friend is here or still out so I walk Gabi to my room. As soon as I close the door to my room, I turn her so she's against the door and begin savoring her. I feel like I've been waiting forever to finally get her here. I lick her mouth...when she opens on a moan, I dive right in. I'm kissing her long and hard. I keep kissing her, then break away and kiss her jaw. Once I've reached her neck, I take a gentle suck that elicits another moan from Gabi. I begin walking slowly to my bed and once there return to kissing her passionately. "I've wanted to get you out of this dress since you opened your door. Can I?"

She breaths out. "Please do."

I can't get this damn dress off of her fast enough. I turn her so I can unzip the dress and place it over the chaise lounge.

I noticed the bustier while unzipping the dress, but I almost swallow my tongue when I see her standing there in front of me in a beautiful white lace bustier with a garter belt and thong, in thigh-high stockings.

"Babe, you – you – I'm at a loss for words – you're stunning. I'm glad that I didn't know that you had this on under this dress all night. Our dinner would have been the fastest dinner ever, we would have beat the world record if there is one."

I take off my jacket, then lay her down on the bed.

"Damn Gabi, you've got to know that this means everything to me. I feel like I've known you all my life. I know that you're not someone who sleeps around, and the fact that you're here with me, right now, in this moment, I'm honored."

I can't wait another second; I've got to go back to kissing this woman. Her lips are soft and are made for me. I cradle her neck and thread my fingers into her hair. I start the deep, drugging kiss that transports both of us to another place. She's moaning and I'm beyond hard.

I begin kissing her neck then slowly pull down on her bustier to reveal the most beautiful nipple that I've seen in my life. It's a dusty caramel, hard and ready for my mouth. She's a perfect D cup. I take a long hard suck, make a soft nip and swirl of my tongue before releasing. I move to her other breast and give it to the same treatment.

I feel a shiver run through her but I'm not nearly done. I begin to move down her body and stop at her belly button for a quick kiss.

Gabi

"Ummm, Jake, you don't have to do what you're about to do." I can tell where Jake is headed. I know that most women love it when a man goes down on them. I haven't had many boyfriends but I never have had a climax this way. I know what my issue is, and it doesn't fall all on the guy...I'm not able to get out of my own head or turn off my brain. I'm always worried about whether he's going to like the taste, will he enjoy it, or am I taking too long to get to the promise land.

"What are you talking about? It's absolutely vital that I do what I'm about to do. I should be embarrassed with how much I've been fantasizing about going down on you since the night that we met."

"I – I've never been able to get there with a guy doing that."

"If that is the case, those other guys didn't know what they were doing. Let me take care of you, baby."

"Ok, but don't get upset if this doesn't end well."

He just chuckles and continues his path to my center.

I feel Jake pulling my underwear to the side and his breath. When I start wondering what's taking him so long, he takes a long swipe up with his tongue and stops at my clitoris which is throbbing in anticipation. He doesn't disappoint. He sucks my clit which lights me up. He adds his finger while tightly swiping his tongue in a rhythm that has me already about to come. I feel him add another finger and begin stroking in and out. He's established a rotation that has me about to lose my mind. Apparently, he has the map to my body because he knows exactly what to do, what I need, and the right amount of pressure to apply.

It doesn't take much more time and before I know it, I'm screaming, "Jake – oh my god, oh my god, I'm coming, don't stop, don't stop, don't stop." My climax hits me like a freight train and feels so amazing. All I can think is 'WOW' so much better than ED (my electronic device).

Jake is inching up my body with a satisfied, cocky grin on his face...he should be, he earned it.

"Jake, I have no words. I swear at one point I left my body."

"Is that a good thing?"

"It's better than good. That was amazing. If I didn't know better, I'd swear someone gave you a cheat sheet because you knew exactly what I needed."

I reach down to stroke Jake to find him straining against his pants. He lets me take the time to rub while admiring his impressive size.

"Let me return the favor," I say.

Jake

I move her hand away. Tonight is not about me, it's about her. I'm in this for the long haul, not a quick lay. This is the first step in my plan to make her see that she should take a chance with me. I don't know if she's ever dated outside of her race, but frankly I don't give a shit if I'm the first white guy that she's dated. I ache for this girl with my entire being.

I lie down beside her and kiss her with so much emotion if my head wasn't already where my heart is, it would scare the hell out of me. I know that she can taste herself on my lips. When I hear her moan again, I damn near change my mind about driving as deep as possible into her.

I stop before I'm unable to and lay her head down on my shoulder. I settle in and pull her close so I can cuddle with her. Strange, I've never been a cuddler, but with her, I like finding every opportunity to hold her in my arms.

I feel Gabi move and notice that an hour has passed. We must have dozed off.

"Babe, you don't have to rush off. You can spend the night if you like."

"No, I better head to my room. I didn't let my friend know that I wouldn't be back tonight and she'll be worried."

"Ok – let me walk you back."

"Jake, you don't have to walk me back. You're apparently as tired as I am."

"This is not up for discussion. I'll be the one who will be worried if I don't know with one hundred percent certainty that you made it back safely."

I help her get dressed, then we're headed to her room.

I give her a quick kiss and leave while I still can. "Goodnight, Gabi. I'll see you tomorrow. Let me know if your plans need to change. I'm flexible and will work around your schedule."

"Goodnight, Jake."

Chapter 6

Jake

The sun is shining brightly into the living room of my suite. The pictures on the website didn't do this room justice. The living room is large enough to have a full-size light gray sofa and matching love seat with blue throw pillows. The room is tastefully decorated and reminds me of my place back home.

I just finished talking to my mom and dad when Travis, my best friend since high school walks into the room. We played on the same junior varsity soccer team in high school. Travis is six foot three with blond hair and played soccer well enough to earn a full scholarship at University of Texas. He still finds time to play on the Houston soccer city league which keeps his muscular form looking like he lives in a gym.

"Man, I've barely seen you all cruise. What have you been up to?" asks Travis.

My instinct is to keep Gabi to myself, but I trust Travis.

"I've met a girl, but not just any girl. She's the one, man."

"Wow! Really – are you sure? Remember what happened with Shelly."

"That was over five years ago. Believe me, I know the difference. I knew it from the moment that I laid eyes on her. We both were at that bar located on the Promenade deck in the middle of the ship. The bar ended up getting stuck for like thirty minutes, which worked in my favor. I was able to get her talking. When she went to leave, I knew that I couldn't leave it up to chance that I would see her again on this ship. I stopped her by grabbing her arm. As soon as I touched her, I felt something at the molecular level. I'm telling you; it was instantaneous. This girl is truly amazing. She's smart, beautiful and down to earth. I find myself being more open, and truly talking to her. She's coming over today for lunch. If you're around, you can meet her."

Before Travis speaks, I see his facial expression. He goes from shocked to reflective. I can tell that he's weighing what he's going to say.

"I've never heard you this into someone before, not even Shelly, and you were engaged to her. I remember when you said you were going to propose to that girl. I tried to talk you out of it. All the reasons that you gave me had to do with the amount of time that she had hung in there with you and it being the next step in your relationship. Never about love. I should have tried harder to talk you out of that disaster. I just may stick around to meet this mysterious woman. Does she have a name?"

"Her name is Gabi. She's a little shy and definitely would rather sit with a good book then go to a nightclub. She's an analyst for a venture capitalist firm, graduate from Harvard and her godfather was awarded a Nobel Peace Prize."

"I know why you're giving me her background. I'm sorry that I'm always looking out for the gold-diggers, but it's in your best interest that someone is looking out for you."

Without Travis having my back, I may have started dating some women who would act very sweet and pretend to be the perfect...fill in the blank...hostess...supportive girlfriend. Somehow Travis always knew the true woman behind the mask. He'd warn me about who she really was and it was never the woman that she was trying to portray to me or the world. Knowing that Travis has my back is important to me. "I do appreciate it, really I do, but it's not necessary."

COULD THIS BE LOVE

"HI, GORGEOUS."

Once Gabi's in the living room, I lean down and give her what I hope is a "you don't realize how much I missed you" kiss. She melts into me and I lean a little bit further forward with her in my arms as I take the kiss deeper. I reluctantly end the kiss. "How did you sleep last night?"

"Between the wine and orgasm courtesy of you, I slept like a baby."

I notice her take a deep breath and has a slight hesitation so I ask, "Is there anything else?" I'm almost afraid to ask.

She has a sparkle in her eyes when she says, "I loved the pink and white roses."

"Pink and white roses? They were pink and white roses?" I say with a confused look on my face. I ordered a tropical flower arrangement to remind her of our Vespas tour yesterday. I rub the back of my neck while turning my head slightly to look at her.

"Well, I received a flower delivery this morning with your card enclosed, but...but..."

She can't even get the words out because she's laughing and trying to stop but she can't help herself.

I drop my head in my hands and groan "Oh, no...there's more to the story."

"They were beautiful with the one exception. There were...there were...pink penis lollipops on sticks throughout the bouquet."

I'm mortified. "That can't be. That's not what I ordered."

Gabi is now in a full-on laugh with tears streaming down her face. I find I'm laughing along with her. I'm horrified and can't believe this happened. I realize in this moment that being able to live a life with Gabi in it would make me a very happy guy.

45

Gabi

This balcony is magnificent with a full-size table that seats eight, four chaise lounges, and a covered loveseat with a canopy for shade. I'm beyond ecstatic that I said 'yes' to lunch. Not only is the view spectacular but I'll have an opportunity to spend more time with Jake.

To my surprise, there's a spread on the table with fruit and meat trays; plus, a guacamole station with chips; and a beverage station with water, soda, champagne and orange juice if I want a mimosa. I feel Jake gently pull me to his back and ask me in my ear "what do you think? Is there something else that you'd like me to order for you?"

"Oh God no – this is more than enough. When you mentioned having lunch, I imagined maybe a hamburger and fries, not a buffet. This is too much, but I must say that I'm very impressed. You did good, McAdams."

I feel him smiling against my cheek. I love that he's so affectionate. I don't think that I have had someone who enjoyed holding me as much as it appears that he does.

He pulls out my chair so I'm facing the ocean. It's the perfect spot since it's in the shade and not too windy.

"What would you like to start with?"

"How about a mimosa?"

"Coming right up."

I take a moment to enjoy the view. This is what a vacation feels like. I truly didn't realize how not taking time off for a real vacation was starting to wear on me. I'd fallen into the routine of taking a random Friday off or adding an extra day off during the holiday. I'm pulled from my thoughts when I hear Jake returning to the table with my drink.

"Yum, this is good and the perfect blend. Thank you."

"Babe, I'll be right back. I think that I heard my phone ding and want to make sure that it's not my parents."

"Take your time." When Jake leaves, I notice that he is playing a mix on his Bluetooth speakers low in the background so I decide to just relax and be in the moment.

I broke my promise to not look him up on the internet. His dad owns a prestigious architectural firm, and his mom was mentioned on several boards. Just when I'm starting to recall the write-up on one of her most recent charities, I hear a knock behind me so I turn and see an unfamiliar man wearing a polo shirt and a polite smile. "Hello, may I help you?"

"I just wanted to stop by and say hello. I'm Travis, a friend of Jake's."

"Hi, Travis. I'm Gabi. How are you enjoying the cruise so far?"

"This is my second cruise, but the first time on a ship this size. I'm enjoying this cruise much better. There's more than enough to keep me busy. How about you?"

"I'm having a great time. This is my first time on a ship this size as well. I'm amazed at the number of things that can be done without even leaving the ship."

"Jake tells me that you're a venture capitalist. How do you like it?"

"I enjoy it, but I put in long hours. It's not uncommon to put in a twelve-plus hour day."

"It sounds like hard work. I can see why you're putting in those types of hours. I'm a corporate attorney specializing in intellectual property."

"We partner with intellectual property attorneys on our deals. It's crazy how easy we can slip into talking about work, isn't it?" I shake my head. "Enough shop talk, we're on vacation. Any plans today?"

"I'm watching the poker tournament. One of the participants made it to the poker championship in Las Vegas."

Jake

I walk out onto the balcony and see Travis talking to Gabi. "Hey, man, I didn't hear you come back in. I see that you met Gabi."

I jerk my head back. I see the glint in Travis's eyes. He knows that I want him to leave now.

"Gabi, I'm getting the boot. It was a pleasure meeting you. Hopefully, I'll have another opportunity to see you before the end of the cruise." He bends to kiss Gabi on her hand. I know that he's doing it to yank my chain. He better not linger too long or I swear that I'm going to kick his ass later.

He's smirking when he straightens. He knows that I know exactly what he was doing. I take my two fingers and point at my eyes then point them to him. For good measure, I take my index finger and slowly go across my throat. He knows I'm not playing with him.

Gabi giggles. "Bye, Travis, it was nice meeting you as well."

"OK, GABI, LET ME MAKE sure that I heard you right. You grew up in New Orleans, then moved to Houston with your parents and grandparents after Hurricane Katrina. Remember when I said that I grew up in the same town where I now live....you're not going to believe it, but it's Houston. My parents live near Rice University. I live in a condo downtown, so I'm close to the office."

"What a small world. My parents live in Montrose. They chose that area because the homes reminded them of New Orleans. Now that you mention it, I've heard a southern accent at times, but not all the time."

"I've tried hard to remove my accent especially since we have clients all over the world. I've found that it helps when communicating with people where English may not be their first language. Where do you work? Are you still in Houston?"

"No, I live in Austin now, but I visit my family frequently. There's always a family gathering, concert, or social gala that my mom wants me to attend. I find that I'm in Houston at least once a month."

This little tidbit of news makes me very happy. Gabi may not realize it yet, but I'm not going to let a little distance cause me to lose touch with her after this cruise. "Tell me more about your family gatherings."

Gabi's eyes sparkle as she smiles brightly. "The St. Claire's are a rowdy, loving bunch. Even though some of us are scattered throughout Texas due to Hurricane Katrina, we make a point to get together every four to six weeks. We always have a ton of food that can range from creole to Italian. Between the food and desserts, no one ever leaves hungry."

Gabi pauses and I can tell that she's reminiscing so I wait.

"It's loud and filled with love. We have games for every age group. The men love to play dominoes, spades or horseshoes. The women usually play a card game like gin rummy. Since my parents' backyard is huge with plenty of room once the music starts playing it's not uncommon to see my grandparents dancing. They love zydeco music."

"Your family sounds amazing. I can't imagine how it was to have to uproot."

"It has been hardest on my grandparents. They have some friends that they haven't seen since before the flood."

"I'm so sorry to hear that. My grandmother's friends are her circle. They find a way to take a day trip usually to a nearby town like Kemah or Galveston. I know that my grandmother would be lost without them, especially now. Can I get you anything else?"

"No, I'm stuffed. I can't eat another bite."

I stand and offer my hand.

"Come here, baby. I've wanted to sit with you in the love seat. It has a phenomenal view of the ocean."

I get her settled, then sit back on the pillows. I've learned a lot about Gabi this afternoon, and all of it is good news for me. I can't believe that her family is in Houston which is my good fortune. I wouldn't have cared if she lived two thousand miles away. I would have found a way to get to her. Two hundred miles is nothing.

I must kiss her before we leave. I turn her around halfway as I give her a light kiss. Before I know it, I've turned her completely to where she's now draped over my lap. I've placed my fingers in her hair to control the kiss and kiss her the way that I dreamed last night. I don't know what it is about Gabi, but I'm not able to go a day without kissing her. Every time I kiss her, I learn something new. She's making this soft hum like I'm a tasty treat. I feel the same way. She tastes like honey from the mini desserts and a sweet nectar that I'm having a hard time naming. I'm quickly becoming addicted to her. I reluctantly pull away from her and look at her expression to see if she's as affected by the kiss as I am.

We sit and just enjoy the view. After some time has passed, I look down and realize that Gabi's appointment is in fifteen minutes. We jump up, grab Gabi's wristlet and walk/jog as fast as we can to the spa while laughing. I'm having the best time of my life.

WE MAKE IT TO THE SPA with minutes to spare. I give her another kiss but before I go and remind her about our date tonight.

"Don't forget that tonight is our *Star Trek* movie date. The movie starts at eight thirty. I was thinking that we could have a casual dinner tonight. I found a pizza spot that makes wood fired pizza and offers some great craft beer. This would allow us to dress casually. How does this sound?"

"It sounds heavenly. What time do I need to be ready?"

"How about seven thirty? This will give us time to grab a quick bite then secure our spot for the movie."

"I love that you're a planner Jake. I'll be ready."

She doesn't have any idea how far my plans go when it comes to her. I'm taking my plans all the way to the altar, kids, grandkids, and old age.

COULD THIS BE LOVE

Gabi

As I walk into the spa reception area, I immediately notice the sound difference. The outdoor sound of guests passing as they head to their own destination disappears. All I can hear is the water feature that covers the entire back wall of the reception counter and the Zen-like music. The walls are tan with a large sea shell-shaped amber chandelier that serves as the central focal point. I finally spot Sam who has already checked in.

"Gabi, this is the best idea. Getting these foot massages with hot stones is right on time," says Sam.

"I'm with you Sam. I wore some high heels last night before the night was over, I totally had to take them off, girlfriend."

"What did you end up doing after dinner?"

"Jake surprised me with this jazz club that played all the old standards. We had a very nice time – I'm amazed by how easy it is just being with him. He's an amazing dancer. I couldn't believe that he booked a private booth, plus had wine and flowers as a finishing touch."

"Gab, I don't want to freak you out, but you seem very happy."

I take a huge breath and exhale. "Sam, I'm afraid to talk too much about him. I don't want to jinx whatever this is. This may sound crazy, especially after my man hiatus, but I'm thinking about spending the night with him tonight. He wanted me to stay last night, and I used you as an excuse on why I couldn't stay."

"Gab, after your last dick wad, I want to see you happy. I say go for it. You only live once."

"You're right, Sam. Even though Dr. Robinson said that there may not be anything wrong, that phrase has a new meaning, I'm going to take a leap and not overthink this."

"That's my girl. Anyway, you need to catch up with me. I slept with Derek on the first night and it was hot as well. I've been able to go back for seconds and thirds."

I laugh because Sam has always been the wild child. This is one of the things that I love about her. I live vicariously through her. She does things that I wish I could do but I'm not as brave as she.

AS WE WALK BACK TO our room, I'm more relaxed after this spa experience than from similar experiences on dry land. It probably has to do with not having to turn around, get in my car, and fight traffic to get back home.

"Sam, what was your favorite service today?"

"My ninety-minute massage was heavenly. I may go back and schedule another session before the end of the cruise."

"Same for me...My masseuse used melted wax to massage me. The wax turned into a warm oil that was incredible. The pressure that she applied lulled me to sleep. I wouldn't be surprised if I wasn't snoring girl – it was just that good. I forgot to ask, what are you and Derek getting into tonight?"

"We're grabbing dinner in the main dining room then will catch the diving show. What about you? I mean besides riding Jake."

"Now you've got jokes. Well, this is going to crack you up. He talked me into going to the movie under the stars tonight. He shared that he's a huge *Star Trek* fan and wait for it – they're playing a *Star Trek* movie tonight. I'm trying to keep an open mind – I did say I was going to try new things, so here's me stepping outside of my comfort zone."

"I'm proud of you, Gab. You're glowing, and my guess is that it's not all from today's spa day. I'm going to have to meet this Jake so I can thank him myself."

"About that, there's something that I may have left out."

"What's that, don't tell me, let me guess – he's shorter than you."

"No silly, it's not anything as tragic as that. Actually, he's white."

"Gab, I've told you a million times, especially after dick wad. I don't care if the next guy that you fall in love with is green. As long as he loves and cherishes you, he's all right in my book."

"I didn't say anything about love, Sam. Why would you say love? I've only known the guy like three days. My god, Sam, you know I've sworn off love."

"Hey...Hey...Gab. Damn, girl, now breathe...in and out, there you go...in and out. I'm just saying if it goes in that direction. Give the guy a chance. Will you promise me that you will?"

"Yes, of course, I will. I'm not stupid, but I'm going on record that it will be a long shot if anything remotely like that happens."

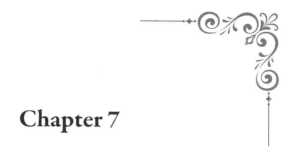

Chapter 7

Gabi

I decide to wear capris, a pink halter top, and my cute summer sandals with the bling. With the matching blingy ponytail holder and natural makeup with pink undertones, the look is pulled together. I usually worry about my height and try to wear heels as much as possible. Jake doesn't appear to care that I'm height challenged.

I hear the knock at my door and look at my watch. It's seven thirty on the dot. Jake is always punctual, which I appreciate.

I open the door to find Jake wearing khakis and a pink polo shirt. I better look in the mirror again to make sure that I'm not drooling. I love a man who will wear pink. It portrays a man who is confident and knows the color doesn't make the man. His muscles are on full display. The shirt is deliciously stretched but not too tight and tapers to his trim waist. I've felt his muscles whenever we've kissed and he's held me but seeing this new side to him, I must say that this look is my favorite.

Jake

I stop in my tracks when I see Gabi in her capris and halter top. She looks sexy as hell. Now that she's gotten a few days of sun, she's a nice golden caramel. My heart is beating stronger since she opened the door. I'm falling for her for real and there's nothing that I can do to fight it. I slowly step inside and close the door. "Hey beautiful, how was your spa day?"

"It was amazing. I wasn't sure what to expect...the reviews gave the staff high marks on this ship and my therapists didn't disappoint...definitely exactly what I needed."

"I see that you received the flower arrangement that I ordered."

"Yeah, it was here when I arrived and the roses were gone. They are beautiful Jake. They remind me of the flowers that we saw on yesterday's excursion. Thank you."

"No, thanks required." I pull Gabi into my arms and dive right in for the kiss that I've been wanting all afternoon, but don't stop there. Before I know it, I've pulled her leg over my hip. My arousal went from zero to a hundred after seeing the outfit that she has on now. I find myself slowly grinding into her. I love the way she's into this as much as I am.

I stop and take a moment to just breath. I just need a minute to get myself back to together. This outfit is revving me in so many ways. If I didn't know better, I'd swear that this girl is trying to give me a heart attack. I notice that Gabi is trying to catch her breath which is satisfying to know that I'm not alone. She may think that this is just chemistry but this is more than that for me.

"Sorry about that, but I couldn't resist. I thought last night's outfit was my favorite but I've changed my mind. This outfit now tops the list."

"Getting ready for tonight was fun. The best part was not having to dress up. It's nice being able to take a break from heels."

WE WALK INTO THE PIZZERIA that has brick walls, dark wood floors, with an exposed ceiling that shows the industrial duct work. I'm going to have to thank Travis. This is the perfect spot for a date with Gabi. He shared that it reminded him of a pizzeria in Boston, Mass and not a restaurant on a cruise ship...he got it right. The music that's playing is great mix. We have heard Maroon 5, Coldplay, Beyonce, and Bruno Mars all while we've been sitting here.

"How's your pizza?"

"Oh my god – this is the best pizza that I've ever had. How did you find out about this place? I don't remember seeing this place listed."

"Travis discovered this spot. He's been hanging out with the guys from the volleyball game. One of the guys is a lawyer like he is, so they've been bouncing strategies off each other."

"You're going to have to thank him from me. This spot gets five stars hands down from me."

I looked down and realized that we better head to the pool deck if we're going to get a seat for the movie.

THE POOL DECK HAS A good crowd tonight for the movie and it's the perfect night. The sky is clear and the stars are shining brightly. The chairs have been arranged in a semi-circle with staggered rows to ensure that everyone has a great view of the screen.

I've dated in high school, college, and after my fiancé Shelly. I can honestly say that I enjoy just being in Gabi's presence. I still can't tell if Gabi thinks this is only a cruise fling. This is so far from a fling to me. I have no doubt in my mind that I'd ask her to marry me now if I thought that she would say yes. I can't wait to tell Jacqi about Gabi. She is going to love her too and has always wanted a little sister.

Gabi pulls me from my thoughts. "I've never watched a movie outside."

"I just hope you like it. I promise not to recite some of the lines."

"You're really that much of a *Star Trek* fan?" Jake blushes a little. "Well, I've been forewarned. You do you, Jake. One of my pet peeves is when a person isn't being authentic. I'd rather see the real you and not a veiled version of yourself."

"I can honestly say that being myself is very natural when I'm with you. I feel light and unencumbered when I'm around you, which is so refreshing. I don't know if I'm making any sense, but I am able to just be with you without any expectations."

Gabi

I wonder if he's talking about the expectations that come with being a McAdams. I can understand having grown up with a family of high achievers with generations of doctors, lawyers, professors and authors. My parents weren't overbearing, but the expectations were clear that anything less than excellence would be a disappointment.

I USUALLY DON'T LIKE movies with aliens. This movie had a great storyline, just the right amount of action, a hot hero, and humor.

"Gabi, what did you think? You looked like you enjoyed the movie."

"I didn't know what to expect but I'm surprised that I liked the movie. I'm hoping that there's a sequel."

Jake looks shocked.

"I'm kidding, even, I know that there was a sequel."

He just shakes his head and squints his eyes. He looks so yummy in this moment.

"We'll have to see if they have it on demand so we can watch it before the cruise ends."

He definitely wants to spend more time with me. I'm not sure what it all means, but I promised myself that I'm going to live in the moment. I'm having a great time, and I'm not ready for this to end.

"Oh, look, they're setting up with a DJ. What do you say? Want to show me what you've got?"

The songs are line dances that are on rotation at my family gatherings. I'm shocked, but Jake knows them and has some moves. I'm having a ball and love whenever Jake pulls me into his side to whisper something in my ear. It's usually something that makes me laugh. Before I know it, I'm getting ready to tell Jake that I need a break.

"Do you need anything?"

This man – he's so observant.

"Yes, I need some water."

He leads me off to find a spot that's out of the way. The crowd is larger than when we first started.

"Would you like anything else – dessert?"

"Ice cream sounds really good right now."

"Let's head to the ice cream parlor. I may get a sundae myself."

We're in luck the line isn't long before I know it, they are taking our order. I can't resist getting a scoop of vanilla with caramel swirl on a sugar cone and Jake gets a two-scoop sundae with caramel drizzle and mini chocolate chips.

The DJ is playing reggae music when we return. It's a great mix. I'll have to see if Jake will dance after we finish our ice cream.

"Yummmm." I close my eyes and savor the ice cream. It tastes amazing, especially in the night air. I'm almost done when I notice Jake's heated gaze is watching my lips intently as I enjoyed the ice cream. He shifts slightly in his seat, so I deliberately take one last long swirl of my tongue before taking my time with swallowing. I swear that I hear a low moan but can't be sure over the sound of the ocean.

I decide to put Jake out of his misery and ask. "Do you see something that you want?"

"Gabi, you know that is a loaded question."

I chuckle – I've never been one to flirt, but I feel so free right now – I'm having the time of my life.

I finish my ice cream then ask. "Well, big boy, what are you going to do about it?"

He has me out of my seat before I can count to two. I'm giggling and very proud of myself that I've gotten him to this point. We're both eager. We're walking fast and don't waste any time getting to his room.

Jake

Sitting there watching her eat her ice cream was torture and so damn erotic. I'm hot and painfully hard. I'm usually very calculated, but with Gabi, it's on another level. We're in my bedroom in record time.

"You do realize that I'm a man on the edge."

She's smiling sweetly with a very satisfied look on her face.

"Let me make it up to you."

Before I know it, Gabi is kneeling in front of me and is running her fingers lightly over my fly. I'm getting harder by the moment. She proceeds to slowly unzip my khakis. I'm so hard right now that I'm surprised, she can get the zipper down. She finally gets me free and begins to slowly rub me up and down while lightly grabbing my balls, which feel so heavy.

"Gabi, please have mercy."

"Now, what's the fun in that Jake?"

She takes me in her mouth and does this thing with her tongue that makes me damn near black out. She's moaning and really into giving me the best head that I've had in my life. Oh, no, I can feel that I'm about to come. I pull out of Gabi's mouth because the first time that I come will not be in her mouth.

"What – what's wrong? Didn't you like it?"

"Baby, if you think the first time that I come with you will be in your mouth, you've lost your mind."

I lift her and begin kissing her with a ferocity that has me groaning. She's kissing me back with everything that she's got. I'm quickly realizing that I've met my match. I thread my fingers into her hair and begin kissing her earlobe, then her neck. I find just the right spot because I feel Gabi tremble, so I do it again. I begin slowly untying her halter top and let it drop to the floor. Her breasts are heavy and her nipples are hard. I bend and take one nipple in my mouth then pull back to swirl my tongue and blow on her nipple. I treat the other nipple the same way. I can't wait any longer, I need to get her in the bed *now*. I carry her to the bedside.

"Jake, there's something that I need to tell you. I've never done this with anyone, I mean sleeping with someone that I've only known for three days. I'm pretty sure that my earlier behavior may have given you a different impression of me but I haven't had a partner in over two years."

I'm shocked that, as beautiful as she is, she doesn't have men lined up and more surprised that someone hasn't already put a ring on it. Those other guys were suckers because I'm not only going to put a ring on it but I'm going to give her the world.

"I'm glad that you let me know. I was already going to take my time but I'll be extra careful."

Gabi

Jake kisses me again and begins to unzip my capris. When he places his hand under my waistband, I'm near panting. I remember how good it felt last night that I can barely wait. He goes right where I want him. He takes a finger and enters me. I should be embarrassed that I'm so wet, but he's making me feel so good I can't think straight. He adds a second finger and I begin to move with his movements. I can tell that I'm close. While pumping me with his fingers, he goes back to my clit. I love a man who can multi-task.

"Jake, I'm coming!" The climax is so long and intense I see stars. When I land back on earth, Jake has a satisfied smile on his face. "You have on too many clothes."

"I can fix that right now."

He stands and takes off his shirt. Oh boy, I knew that he was fit, but he has a six pack that I'm definitely going to have to explore before the night is over. Just when I didn't think that it could get any better, he takes off his pants and boxers. I just had him in my mouth but I swear that his member has gotten bigger and is now pointing up towards his stomach. I'm not having second thoughts, but he's bigger than any of my other partners.

"I'm not sure if you're going to fit."

"Oh, we'll fit. Don't worry baby, I'm going to take my time. I'm not in any hurry. We have all night."

Jake

I can tell that Gabi is nervous, and I want her more than ready. I pull her to the edge of the bed and drape her legs over my shoulders. I begin kissing her inner thigh and enter her with two fingers and slowly pump while sucking on her clit. I get into a good rhythm and Gabi begins to ride my face. I flick my tongue rapidly as she begins to climb. I can tell that she's close. I take her clit and begin pulling and retreating while sucking. She bows her back but I don't let up. I want her to ride this climax as long as possible. I slowly let her come back down and settle her back in the middle of the bed.

I put on my condom so damn fast that I know that I look eager.

"Gabi – look at me."

She slowly opens her eyes. She already looks satisfied but I still see the fire there. I begin to push slightly. When Gabi's eyes open in alarm, I stop pushing and slowly pull almost all the way out.

"Baby, I promise that I won't hurt you."

She nods so I begin again by pushing in part of the way and pulling back slightly. I continue to do this until I'm finally all the way in. She is so damn tight. If I didn't already know that she was made for me, this would have sealed it. Being inside of her is like nothing that I've ever felt. I feel this down to the depths of my soul. I already knew that she's the one. I have no doubt that she was made for me. I begin to move, taking my time to ensure I don't hurt her.

I bend to suck one of her hard nipples while continuing to pump into her. I can feel that she's getting wetter so I pick up the pace. I hold down her hip as I continue to move into her with deep, slow precision. I find her g-spot and hit it over and over until I feel her contract against me. I'm so damn close, but ladies first. I reach down and begin flicking her clit until she was coming with a vengeance. I follow right after her and continue to pump into her until I have nothing left.

I lift to keep my weight off of her and kiss her forehead. I pull out gently to ensure that I don't cause any pain and to take care of the condom.

It looks like she's asleep when I walk back into the room, so I try to get into the bed without waking her. I pull her into my arms and fall asleep by the time my head hits the pillow.

Chapter 8

Gabi

G abi
  I wake wrapped in Jake's arms. He's not up yet but another part of him is. We had another round in the middle of the night, so I'm surprised that he's ready to go again.

Jake kisses my shoulder and sleepily says "Ignore him. He'll be all right. What can I do for you this morning? Want me to order some breakfast?"

"Let me text my girlfriend to see what she decided to do today."

Gabi: Hey Sam – just waking up, do you have plans today?

Sam: Yes, Derek and I are getting off the ship to walk around for a bit. Get in all the Jake time you can.

Gabi: Thanks sis. xoxo

I turn to Jake. "She plans to spend the day with Derek. I'm all yours, but there's a slight problem. I need to take a shower."

"Well, well, look who hit the jackpot – I need to take a shower too and I have a full-size shower. Will you join me, my lady?"

"I'd love to, kind sir." I can't recall when I've ever been able to be silly with the opposite sex. My serious side is always present no matter how hard I try to relax and be in the moment.

He bows and holds his hand out for me. I'm still smiling as we walk into the bathroom. It's huge and decorated with white subway tile, chrome accents, and industrial lighting, plus has a double sink. The shower is large enough for two adults with room to spare.

Jake

After the water is warm enough, I help Gabi into the shower. She grabs the soap and begins to get a good lather. I'm expecting her to begin soaping herself. No, my girl turns with a sly smile on her face and begins to grab me in a loving touch. I'm back to rock hard in seconds.

"Babe that feels good – just like that. Oh, that feels good, real good."

She begins to pump faster, over and over, then she caresses my balls with the other hand, squeezes with enough pressure that has me erupting. I finally stop and have to catch my breath.

I grab her and kiss her with everything that I've got. With her against the wall and away from shower head, I don't know what she expected but she is surprised when I kneel down. I drape one of her legs over my shoulder and begin to eat her like she's my first meal in a week. Her taste is addictive. She has the sweetest pussy that I've ever tasted and I go to town on her. It doesn't take long before she's screaming and coming hard.

When we both come down from our high, I say, "I swear that I didn't suggest a shower together expecting anything."

"What can I say, I couldn't help myself."

Once we dry off, I give Gabi a t-shirt and pair of my basketball shorts. She's drowning in them but looks so cute. I know that I'll remember this image for the rest of my life. I put on some jogging pants and a t-shirt. If it was just me and Gabi, I'd go sans shirt. I can tell that she loves looking at me because I've caught her shy glances. I love her looking at me, so it's a win-win.

"I'm not sure if Travis is here or not. Any issues if he joins us for breakfast?"

"None whatsoever. I like Travis."

We walk out of my room when I see Travis crossing the living room.

"Hey, Jake, I was wondering if you were still here. What did you get into last night...Oh, hi Gabi! Good morning!" I hear him chuckle. He knows that I'll be pissed if he makes a crude remark about me hooking up with Gabi.

"We were just about to order some breakfast. Would you like to join us?" asks Jake.

"No, I was heading out for the day. I'm playing golf with the guys we met at the volleyball game. Have fun, kids." says Travis.

"What do you have a taste for today?" asks Jake.

"I think that I'll just have an egg-white omelet with spinach and tomatoes, plus a fruit salad."

Gabi

We decide to eat on the balcony. I'm soaking in every last moment, and this view is one of them. I can't believe how fast time is flying by. I'm really enjoying Jake's company. He is so easy to be around. Too bad that we won't be seeing each other after the cruise. I'm not fooling myself. I don't know if he's ever dated a Black girl, and I'm not going to ask. Even though this is the 2000s, racism still exists. Dating me would not be an easy path for him to take, and I do not get the impression that Jake has had to face much adversity in his life.

No, a cruise fling is definitely what I needed. I've been jumping from project to project for practically three years straight that I hadn't realized that I had a nonexistent personal life, never mind not even having a special friend with benefits to blow off some steam with every now and then.

Jake leans over and kisses me between my eyebrows. "What are you thinking about? You have some serious frown lines going on."

I should be open with Jake about my questions on whether we're on the same page about this being just a cruise fling. No, it's best to enjoy today.

"I was just thinking about how I've let work take over my life. It happened so gradually; you know. It began with working a weekend to meet a deadline to working a few evenings a week to working every evening and most weekends."

"I can relate. I work crazy hours as well. If it wasn't for Travis dragging me out to golf or to watch a live sports event, I would work nonstop. My dad has designed some amazing buildings in his lifetime. I wouldn't say that I'm competing with him but I want him to be proud. I hope that doesn't sound juvenile. I know that I'm a grown man, but what he thinks still matters to me."

"Yeah, I understand what you mean. My parents have never put pressure on me to be successful. They just wanted me to find a career that was my passion," says Gabi.

"Do you love what you do?" asks Jake.

"I love the compensation package and the lifestyle. I wouldn't say that it's my passion, though. I'm good at what I do. The issue that I have is I don't know what is the one thing that I would do even if I weren't paid. I'm good with VC for now until I figure it out," says Gabi.

AFTER STOPPING BY MY room so I can change into my swimsuit and the purple sarong that I purchased the other day, we decide to hang out by the pool while I rest. My energy level is zapped, not sure if it's the marathon sex or something else, whatever it is, I'm ready for a nap.

"Do you mind helping me with the sunblock? You wouldn't realize it but I burn very easy," asks Gabi.

"You never have to ask me twice for anything. Turn over," says Jake.

His hands feel amazing. He's applying the right amount of pressure while being thorough. He's revving me up at the same time. Funny how my tiredness is a distant memory in this very moment.

Jake

Having my hands on Gabi feels fucking amazing. The bikini she's wearing is sexy as hell. When she walked out in the deep purple two-piece with the knotted top and high cut bottoms that highlight her legs, I had to do a double take. She's wearing one of the coverups that she purchased the other day. All I could say is 'damn'. You'd think by now that I wouldn't be taken aback by her beauty, especially since I know every inch of her by now. I'm trying to do algebra and trigonometry to keep myself from losing control. My board shorts will not hide my predicament much longer.

Right at that point, I feel Gabi's eyes on me. She gives me a sly smile. She has on her shades, but I'm pretty sure that she sees the battle that I'm quickly losing. Fuck it – I take an extra towel and place it over my lap. She's turned around now, and is full out laughing at this point.

"Go ahead, laugh it up now, but remember this later." I lean over and give her a quick kiss but before I know it, I'm giving her a deep, long kiss. I should be worried that I can't seem to hold back with her. I normally am not this affectionate, but it feels so right that I'm not going to even overthink it.

"I'm sorry, Jake. It's really not funny. Are you sure we don't need to go back to the room to take care of that?"

If I had a short view of where I want our relationship to go, I'd be leading her back to the room so fast we'd be dizzy by the time we got there. No, that's not the play. Today is about just spending time with her.

I decide that I better lay on my stomach while I get myself together. I turn my head so I'm facing Gabi and watch as she puts sunblock on her face, arms and legs. She's singing softly to the Rupert Holmes song that's playing ... "*If you like piña coladas, And gettin' caught in the rain...*" I know the song but I'm just happy listening to her...Gabi has an amazing voice.

GABI AND I HAD A NICE day. After lunch, we headed down to the market so she could get some souvenirs for her family. I grabbed a few bottles of bourbon for my dad and wondered if he'd like Gabi. She's amazing and fits so naturally with me. My dad already knew how frustrated I'd been with the dating scene. The girls are more interested in my status and pedigree than in me. They see the McAdams name and want everything that comes with it (galas, traveling the world, country club, and rubbing elbows with the upper crust of society). I have friends who are looking for trophy wives. I'm looking for someone I can build a life with; someone I can't wait to see and talk about how my day went. Even though Gabi and I have only been together for less than a week, I find myself opening up to her in ways that I don't with anyone, even Travis.

I've just finished grabbing a soda out of the mini bar when Travis walks back in.

"Travis, how was the course?"

"It was amazing. The golf course had just enough complexity to make it challenging. We did eighteen holes, then grabbed lunch in the clubhouse. Bringing my clubs was the best idea, man. Thanks for suggesting it. Even though, I don't need to ask - how was your day with Gabi?"

"What do you mean?"

"You are beaming and look very happy. After the year that you've had, a cruise fling is exactly what you needed."

"If you weren't my best friend, I'd punch you in the nose right now."

"What? Wait a minute, are you saying what I think that you're saying?"

After sitting down and taking a huge sigh, I begin, "I'm pretty damn sure that I'm already head over heels in love with this woman. Before you say anything, I know that you think this is moving way too fast. Believe me that if I had any control over this, I'd pump the brakes a bit, but I can honestly say that I've never felt like this before."

"Are you sure that it's not just because you lost your grandfather a few months ago? You even said that you felt a little off kilter. What if it's because you're vulnerable right now? I can see why you're infatuated with her, she's gorgeous. I just don't want to see you get hurt."

"Yes, she's beautiful, but it's way beyond that. I feel as if I've known her all my life. When I'm around her, I'm so damn calm. Not sure if I can describe it but it's like when you're at work, and you hear constant chatter all around you, then you put on noise-cancelling earbuds. She does that for me. My biggest fear is that I'm going to come off too strong and scare her away. I'm trying my best not to mess this up. I know that I've told you before that I think she's the one. The more time that I spend with her just solidifies for me that she's, my soulmate."

"Wow! I can't say I'm surprised. You look different. Your whole demeanor has changed."

"And the best part is her family lives in Houston and she lives in Austin. This little discovery is confirmation for me that we're destined to be together. After the cruise, I plan to continue what we started."

"When are you seeing her again?"

"We're grabbing dinner at the Italian restaurant, then maybe either salsa dancing or the nightclub that you've been talking about."

"Not sure if I'll see you there. There's a game on tonight, so me and the guys are going to the sports bar then maybe hit the casino. Afterwards, I'm open to another type of extracurricular activity if you know what I mean."

I just shake my head. "I hear you." Travis has always been into the casual thing. I've never found it appealing. Sure, I've dated my fair share of girls and had some one-night stands but prefer to have a girlfriend than a random hookup.

I DECIDE TO GIVE GABI the necklace that I bought for her the other day, the one she'd admired at the jewelry store. They even giftwrapped it for me. I'm not sure what she's wearing tonight but I hope it's an outfit that will go with the pendant.

"Hey, gorgeous."

"Hey yourself. I'm almost ready, and you can meet Sam. Sam, Jake is here."

Samantha walks into room. She a little taller than Gabi with braids and dressed for the evening wearing a red jumpsuit.

Samantha holds out her hand. "Jake, it's nice to meet you. Gabi has had nothing but good things to say about you. What are y'all getting into tonight?"

"We're having dinner at the Italian restaurant then maybe dancing," says Jake.

"Sounds good. I'm headed out myself. It was nice meeting you. Have fun, you two."

Samantha starts to leave when I see her in my peripheral give Gabi a thumbs up.

I step closer to Gabi. "You look amazing. I'm glad that I decided to bring this."

"What are you talking about, Jake?"

Gabi

He hands me a beautifully wrapped box. It feels heavy. I shake the box to see if it will give me a clue. I finally start opening the package. Oh, this is a jewelry box. I slowly open the box to find the most beautiful necklace and I feel my eyes go big. My breath catches and I snatch my eyes up to Jake's, when I remember, this is the purple, amethyst necklace that I saw at the shop. He's watching me intensely to see my reaction.

"Jake, you shouldn't have," I whisper.

"Gabi, I noticed how much you wanted the necklace and had to get it for you."

I could have purchased the necklace but for some reason I have a difficult time splurging on myself. Of course, I had second thoughts but it was too late to go back since the ship had sailed for the next destination. I was disappointed and had planned to look for the pendant at the next stop to see if I could find a similar cut.

"When did you even have time to make the purchase? We were together all afternoon."

"I have my ways and will always find occasions to surprise you."

When he says things like that, he talks as if there's a chance that we will be seeing each other after the cruise, and that he has every intention of seeing me once we're home.

He's moved closer to me and takes the necklace out of the box.

"Turn around, babe. Let's see it on you."

I'm wearing my hair down in a wavy style that falls to my left side. I lift it as I turn so he can fasten the clasp. I watch us in the mirror. The necklace is absolutely gorgeous and goes perfectly with my dress. I had decided to wear a purple and jade maxi dress that cuts in at the shoulders to a high collar and has a slit that shows some cleavage. I caught Jake several times on our first date glancing at my chest. Jake is looking at us now with heat in his eyes. He starts placing kisses on my neck and I feel it all the way down to my toes.

"I love the necklace. It's absolutely beautiful. I'll always remember that you gave this to me. I hope that you know that."

I've never had a guy that I was dating notice that I really admired something and then made a point of buying it for me as a surprise. Their gifts have usually been something that they want to get me because they like it themselves, not because I might like it. There was this guy that bought me a set of golf clubs because he wanted me to golf with him. I didn't even golf at the time and hadn't expressed that I wanted to learn how to golf. Not sure what he was thinking.

I turn to kiss him now and thank him for this gift. I love the way he fists my dress at my lower back. He pulls me harder to him and takes over the kiss. He's hungrily kissing me and has his free hand cradling my head. He's holding my head exactly where I want it to be. I'm being consumed, and I like it. I can't get enough of him. I'm not sure how long we have been kissing when Jake pulls away. He's breathing hard as I am. "Do we need to go? Want to stay in?"

"I'd love to stay in, Gabi. But let's go out. I want to take you to dinner then dancing, plus you've taken the time to get ready. We better go before I change my mind."

AFTER DINNER, WE DECIDE to head to the nightclub instead of salsa dancing. Both Travis and Sam said that the DJ is off the chain.

I'm surprised...I wasn't sure what to expect. The nightclub is more of a lounge with a VIP setting. The room is dark with blue lighting and has a hip, trendy ambiance. Blue velvet love seats with small tables illuminated with sky blue lighting are strategically placed around the room to give couples a view of the dance floor. There are several couples dancing while the DJ spins his records.

"How do you like the music?" asks Jake.

"He has a good mix going."

"Would you like something to drink?"

"How about a Piña Colada?"

"Can we have a Piña Colada and bourbon neat?"

We sit and listen to the music. The DJ is on a roll. He's playing one hit after another with the goal of keeping everyone on the dance floor. I'd just finished my drink when Jake stands.

"Shall we?"

I don't know what to expect when I hear The Weeknd's "Can't Feel My Face" starting. As soon as we hit the floor, Jake starts moving. He has rhythm...line dancing is one thing, but dancing...real dancing...is another. I think of the saying "Watch how a man dances and you'll have a good idea how he'll be in bed." I can testify that this is sage wisdom. Jake has it going on.

When he smiles and looks at me like this, I feel like I'm the only girl in the room. There are a ton of women in here in various degrees of dress, but Jake only has eyes for me. I could really get used to this. After two more songs, a slow song begins. He pulls me right in without any hesitation. I love that he's so confident. We're molded together when he begins to move and starts singing "Perfect" by Ed Sheeran. He has wonderful voice. I feel like I'm in a fairy tale. He makes me feel like a princess who is cherished. How is this even possible?

I'm trying to keep my head on straight. There is nothing that can come from this. This is just a crazy connection that we have while on vacation. Folks do crazy things while on vacation like smoke weed and get their hair braided. That's all this is. Now to keep telling myself this – hopefully, I'll start to believe it and won't get caught up.

Jake

I heard "Perfect." I have always listened to this song in a melancholy mood because I never believed that I would find someone who I felt met the criteria. Now that I've found Gabi, I'm singing this song to her. It's like they wrote this song knowing that I'd be in this exact moment right now with the girl of my dreams. She feels so good in my arms. We're perfect together. I have got to begin working on a plan to keep this girl just like I knew when I first met her that I could not let her walk away. I need to find a way to make Gabi believe that there can be an us.

She gives me a wicked wink. "Jake, would you think less of me if I say that I'm ready to head back to your room?"

This girl – I was thinking the same thing but didn't want to cut the night short if she wanted to hang out longer.

I kiss her temple and place my hand on her lower back as I lead her out of the club. I can feel appreciative eyes on Gabi. I'm not the only one who thinks she's beautiful. I stick out my chest a little bit more. I'm proud to be the one that she chose.

"How does walking outside for a bit sound?"

"I'd like that. I bet the night sky is lit since it's a full moon."

We walk in silence. I notice Gabi shiver, so I take off my jacket and place it around her shoulders. I pull her into my side for good measure. I love having any excuse to have her in my arms. I feel zero shame in capitalizing on the opportunity every chance that I get.

I let us into my room and notice that Travis still isn't back. "Would you like anything to drink? The mini bar stays pretty well stocked. I thought that we could sit on the sofa and listen to some music."

"What do you have?"

"Let's see – there's cranberry juice, fruit juice, vodka, rum."

"You can stop there. I'll take fruit juice with rum."

I turn on a slow mix before I give Gabi her drink and take a seat. "What was your favorite part of today?"

Gabi

"I had several parts but the best was spending time with you and getting this beautiful necklace. I still can't believe that you did that."

"Gabi, I've been wanting to talk to you about some..."

I don't give him a chance to say whatever he's going to say. I'm afraid what it will be. I'm not sure if I'm stopping him from finishing his sentence because I'm more afraid that he's going to say he wants something more or to clear the air to make sure that we're on the same page with this only being a cruise fling.

I put my drink down and take his to place it on the coffee table. I'm straddling him and kissing him. It doesn't take long before Jake is really into this as much as I am and kisses me into next week. He begins to place me on the sofa before he has second thoughts and stands with me wrapped around him. He's kissing me and walking towards his room. I'm beyond grateful that he has his own room.

COULD THIS BE LOVE

Once we're in his room, I unwrap my legs from his waist and begin kissing his jaw, his neck and start pulling his shirt from his pants. I struggle to take off his belt buckle. I want him *now*. I finally get his pants unzipped and off. I push him down on the bed and can tell that I've surprised him. I lay next to him while I stroke him but I've learned not to get him too excited before I go down on him. Jake is a big guy. If I want a head start, I need to take him in my mouth while he'll fit.

I lick the head before sucking him into my mouth. I take as much of him as I can and begin to pull up. Once I get to his head, I repeat the process, over and over until Jake pulls me up with a growl.

Jake

I want to worship her body until she has no doubt that I want more with her. I can tell that I surprised her by stopping her.

"Babe, I love everything that you were doing, but I want tonight to be special. Let me focus on you. It's not about me."

She nods but doesn't say anything.

I start kissing her until she's moving underneath me. I reach down to take her breast in my hand while kissing her neck. I love how her breasts feel in my hand. They have the right amount of heaviness and her nipples slightly point up. I begin to pull one in my mouth and suck while moving my hand down to her mound. She's already wet and coats my fingers. I play with her clit and listen to the moans. She's so responsive to me.

I enter her with two fingers and begin stroking her. I want to make sure that she's more than ready for me. While stroking her, I take my thumb and rub her clit up down until I feel her explode around my fingers. I don't let her get through the first orgasm before I am moving down to taste her. I suck up her juices which are intoxicating. She tastes so good that I want to spend the night down here. I tongue her in and out while alternating between sucking her clit. It doesn't take long before she's starting to peak again.

Gabi grabs my hair and begins losing control. This is what I wanted. I don't want the prim and proper Gabi. I want her out of her mind for me.

"Jake, oh my GOD, oh, oh, oh – I'm COMING. Don't stop. OH MY GOD."

Her climax goes on and on then she drops back to the bed. I've pulled myself back up to the bed by the time she turns to look at me with a sated look on her face. I could beat my chest right now because I'm the one that put that look there.

I grab a condom but Gabi takes it out of hand and rolls me onto my back. After putting the condom on me, she begins to take me inside of her. Once I'm all the way in, she begins to lift up and down, building a rhythm that would rival a rodeo cowgirl. I help her to climax number three.

I've been wanting Gabi from behind since the first night. I lift her off and place her on all fours. Her eyes get big when she sees how much harder I am.

"I promise to take my time." I take my fingers and start at the top of her spine. When I get to her lower back, I caress her ass and begin to push into her from behind. With the three orgasms, she takes me without any issues. I set a pace with long, strong strokes alternating with short, rapid stokes and back to long, strong strokes when I feel the start of my own release. I'm not coming without Gabi falling over the cliff with me. I reach down to her clit and beginning rubbing while I'm pumping into her. She screams out then and grips me like a vice. I take both of my hands and begin pumping into her with everything that I've got.

I come and before I know it, I'm coming again. I hope the condom holds all of it.

I bend to kiss her ass cheek before slowly pulling out to deal with the condom.

COULD THIS BE LOVE

With the condom dealt with, I lift her so she's under the covers and join her. With her back to my front, I'm stroking her hair, kissing her shoulder when I notice that her breathing is even. She's fallen asleep. I fall asleep with a smile on my face because I know that I accomplished my goal of worshiping her.

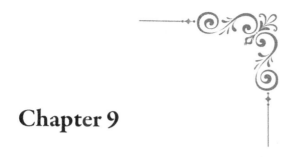

Chapter 9

Gabi

This is the second time that I've woken wrapped in Jake. He's holding one of my breasts. I take the time to enjoy this. Today is the last day of the cruise. I can't believe how fast the week has passed. I'm trying not to be sad about this all coming to an end. Jake is amazing. I do wonder how things would have turned out if our paths had crossed at a festival or restaurant in Texas. Would Jake have been persistent about getting my phone number? Would I have given him my real phone number? Before I can ponder this more, I sense Jake move behind me as he squeezes my breast.

"Hmmmm, Gabi – I need you."

"Well, what's stopping you?"

He turns me and reaches down to see if I'm ready. I'm finding that I'm in a constant state of arousal with this man. He puts on a condom and begins to move. He's got a slow stroke going and is looking at me tenderly. When he looks at me like this, it's like he's seeing me for the first time. I feel like the prettiest girl in the world.

"Gabi, I'm not going to last long and I need you there with me."

He reaches down and begins strumming me with precision. I feel the start of my climax when Jake's strokes become more persistent, stronger, longer, harder – then he's falling over the edge with me.

Jake

You'd think by now that I would have my fill of Gabi. I don't know if I ever will. The more that we make love, the more that I want to make love with her. I take care of the condom, brush my teeth, and come back to find Gabi exactly where I left her. "Do you have anything on your agenda for today?"

"Nothing at all, actually. Sam is going on a rum tour with Derek, so I'm on my own today."

"Are you afraid of heights?"

"I'm not sure. What did you have in mind?"

"I was thinking that we could go parasailing, grab lunch, and walk around town."

"Ooh, I've always wanted to parasail. It sounds like fun. I better head back to my room now so I can check in with my mom and dad before we head out."

I sense that Gabi is trying to put some distance between us. I'll try harder to check myself and make sure I'm not coming on too strong. We'll hang out today and take it easy. I'll let her drive whether we do something this evening. I'll be disappointed but I'll give her space if she wants it. Even with our cruise ending tomorrow, this is just the beginning for us. I just need to show her that we're meant to be together.

Gabi

We have been secured in our parasail harnesses and are beginning our ascent from the back of the boat. I'm excited and enjoying the slight ocean breeze. Once we've made it to the top, I love the view from here. "Look at the view from here. You can see the entire island. This view is beyond majestic. What do you think?"

"The view up here is stunning."

I look over to realize that he's not talking about the island but me. I hold his gaze for a moment, but it's too intense so I breakaway and begin my nervous habit of filling the silence. "Thank you for suggesting this. It's the perfect excursion to end the vacation. The weather is perfect – not a cloud in the sky. And it's just warm enough without the stifling heat."

AFTER PARASAILING, we grabbed lunch at a cantina on the beach and grabbed a few more souvenirs. Neither one of us had started packing for tomorrow's departure so we decided to come back to the ship. I'd just started packing, when Sam walked back into the room.

I'm too anxious to pack so I grab a water and walk over to the sofa with a huff. "Sam, I can't believe that I invited Jake out on a date tonight. Last night and this morning were straight out of a dream. I'd made up my mind, for my own self perseverance, that I need to start pulling away. We've been together every day on this cruise and tomorrow we'll be going to the airport to head home. I felt that it was best to yank off the band-aid even though I know that it's going to hurt like hell. Shit – what am I doing?"

"Gab, no need to panic. I'm proud to see that you've been going with the flow. This vacation did you good. You were so stressed when you first got here that I wasn't sure if you'd be able to relax at all. Jake has been good for you, fling or not. My advice to you is to relax and enjoy tonight. Don't worry about tomorrow. What will be will be. You know your grandmother always talks about fate and destiny."

"No, Sam. Don't say anything else. I'm not sure what this is, but the last thing that I want to do is put something out in the atmosphere. I believe what my grandmother says is true. I just never believed it for me. I've never been someone who has had things fall into her lap. Everything that I've earned, I've worked very hard for it. Why would love be any different? I'm not even sure if I'll ever find the one."

Sam gives me the side eye. She knows that I'm so stressed out right now. I'm surprised that she isn't trying to change my mind.

AFTER PACKING, I START getting ready for dinner. I decide to wear a lilac and baby-blue chiffon floor-length wrap dress that has a plunging neckline and shows a little leg when I walk. I'm glad that I remembered to bring the bra that I need to wear with this dress. I figure this outfit will ensure that Jake doesn't forget me for a little while after the cruise.

As usual, Jake is right on time. I tried to suggest that we just meet at the restaurant, but Jake wouldn't hear of it. I'm surprising him with the Brazilian Steakhouse that's on the ship. I haven't met a man yet that doesn't like the challenge of eating as much beef as possible.

Jake

Gabi opens the door and I almost have a coronary. Her dress is sexy as hell. She's done something different to her hair so it's loose and bouncy. My eyes immediately latch onto her lips and see that she's done something different to them also. They are sparkly and very glossy. She's taller tonight too. I look down and notice that she has on heels that make her legs look amazing. This entire look is smoking hot.

I don't trust myself. I have to clear my throat twice before I can ask, "Are you ready?" I need to get us both from behind closed doors before I'm not held responsible for my own actions.

Before Gabi turns, I see a slight tilt of her mouth. Oh, I see how it is. She meant to turn me inside out. She's thrown down the gauntlet. I've never been one to step away from a challenge. I'm going to love every minute of this.

Folks are already starting to pack for tomorrow's departure and have placed their suitcases outside their door for pickup so I have to take Gabi's hand and walk with her behind me. We finally get to the elevators. Since I don't know where we're going, I let her lead. She presses the button for the floor.

As soon as we arrive, the doors open to a dark burgundy room with waiters dressed in Brazilian garb. They're wearing black pants, black shirt, a red sash and topped off with a red handkerchief tied around their neck. The aroma smells delicious. I know immediately where we're at. I'm impressed that she chose this restaurant. She's a woman after my own heart, and I just found another reason to love her.

We're immediately taken to our seat by one of the waiters. Gabi's leading the way and I love the view. Seeing the sway of her hips is so sensual that I'm counting the minutes until I can have my way with her. I notice an extra swing that I know is only for me. This girl is too much.

I'm smoother this time when I signal the waiter that I've got her chair. I pull it out and dip to whisper in her ear as I push the chair under the table. "How's this?" I make sure that my voice is deeper and laced with need. I'm satisfied when I see her shiver.

"Gabi, I love that you booked dinner for us here. I remember seeing this one listed and thought that it would be fun. I love how they retrieve wine from the glass-enclosed wine cellar. The girls are hooked to wires from the ceiling allowing them to spin at the waist as they are retrieving the wine. I went to a restaurant during one of my conferences in Vegas and was impressed by how it adds to the ambiance."

"You've been doing the heavy lifting all week with securing dinner for us. It's the least that I can do."

We're interrupted for our drink and sides order. I take the time to really admire Gabi's beauty. This dress is super sexy. She's allowing a little thigh to show as she sits. I'm the lucky recipient since the slit falls on my side. I know this little display is for me and I will show my appreciation later. I can tell she really doesn't know how beautiful she truly is, and I'm amazed. I've only scratched the surface in understanding her, and I'm more than motivated to continue my exploration. "What would you like to do our last night on the ship?"

"I was thinking that we could go back to the jazz club. How does that sound?"

"Fantastic." Now I'll have another opportunity to dance with Gabi before the night is over.

Gabi

We arrive to the jazz club when the next set is just starting. There's a male singer tonight who sounds like Michael Bublé and has started with "Fly Me to the Moon," but with a slower, more sensual pace.

Jake stands, "Shall we?"

I smile and place my hand in his. We are next to a middle-aged black couple. The woman makes eye contact with me and looks to Jake then makes a nod. I haven't been looking for approval but it felt good.

He's smooth, how he pulls me into his body. I melt right into him. I'm always amazed when we dance how it feels like we have been dancing together for years. He wraps me in his arms and I place my head on his shoulder just enjoying the moment while trying not to become sad that our time together has to come to an end after tonight.

The next old standard is my favorite, "The Way You Look Tonight." I press closer to Jake and hear him begin to sing in my ear. It's only loud enough for me. The song is almost over when I look up to see Jake looking at me with so much emotion in his eyes. I'm confused because this can't be real, but he's looking at me like I matter to him...like I'm his. This is a crazy, one-week vacation where I've stepped out of my normal existence that I plan to bottle up and keep as a wonderful memory for the rest of my life.

"Jake..." I don't get to say anything before he begins to kiss me softly. He keeps the kiss sweet and light.

"I'm sorry, Gabi. I couldn't not kiss you. This night with you is way past any expectations that I've had in a long time. Thank you."

"For?"

"For just being you." He shakes his head and says again, "Just being you. I want to spend some time alone. Are you ready to call it a night?"

"Thought you'd never ask."

Jake doesn't have to be told twice. He tucks me against his side and begins walking with a purpose. If I didn't want him as much as he wants me, I'd find this funny. He's serious as a heart attack. I'm on the same page and glad to see that he doesn't want to waste any time.

Jake

As soon as we make it to my room, I press Gabi against the door and begin kissing her with a need of a man who is having his last meal. After devouring her mouth, I begin kissing her jaw and move to the spot on her neck that I know makes her moan. She doesn't disappoint. I can't get enough of her and am more determined than ever that we will continue what we've started on this cruise. I'm willing to go as slow as she needs me to, but I'm not known to be a patient man. We will have a relationship. I just need to get her on the same page as me.

I slowly begin moving my hand up the split that has been driving me out of my mind since I picked her up for our date. Her silk panties are wet. I growl and pull them aside as I begin moving one finger inside her. Her juices are flowing. I can tell she's close. I've learned how to angle my fingers so they are hitting her g-spot. I add another finger and begin moving my body as if I'm already inside her.

I have to taste her now before I lose it. I drop to my knees, raise one of her legs, and drape it over my shoulder. Damn, her scent is intoxicating. I don't have time to take her panties off in a civilized manner. I have them ripped before another second passes. I hear Gabi gasp above me. She begins moaning as I take a long swipe of my tongue from her opening up to her clit. I stay with her clit and give it the attention that it's begging for then take her clit in my mouth and begin sucking. This catapults her over the edge. I continue to lick her with a vengeance. I'm nowhere near finished yet. She's going to come against my mouth one more time before I'm in her so deep we won't know where she starts and I end.

I add my fingers again as I go back to flicking her clit. I build her back up but it doesn't take long before she's coming again. As she's coming down, I let her come down slowly. Her scent is continuing to make me crazy. I begin kissing the inside of her thigh and suck a little harder.

I walk Gabi to the bed. When we reach it, I begin taking off her dress. Her bra is a complicated contraption, but I'm nothing if not creative. She takes pity on me, unhooks the bra and lets it fall to the ground. She's now standing in front of me in nothing but those high heels. She bends to take them off, but I stop her.

"No, those stay on." My voice is rougher than I meant it to sound, but I'm hanging by a thread by now. I'm so damn hard right now that I undress, grab a condom, turn Gabi towards the bed and bend her over.

Gabi is looking at me over her shoulder as I finish putting on the condom.

I ask her, "How do you want it? You need to tell me. Do you want me gentle or hard and fast?"

"Hard and fast, Jake...and hurry." She speaks in a voice that is so sexy, I'd do anything to make sure that I could give her everything.

I hold her hips tight. I don't want her to move for fear I might hurt her. Instead of plunging into her like I want to, I slowly stroke in then out until I'm half way in then I plunge the rest of the way. Hell, nothing has ever felt this good.

"Give me a second. I'm about to blow and I want this to last."

"Move, Jake. Now, Jake. I want it all. Don't hold back."

She gave me the permission that I needed. I begin fucking her. It feels so good. I'm long stroking her now and feel her begin to get wetter so I do it again.

"Oh damn, oh shit, Gabi, this feels so good."

I can tell I'm hitting her g-spot so I reach down and begin playing with her clit. Gabi is coating me with her juices. Her contractions feel so good that my orgasm sneaks up on me and I see stars.

I lean forward to catch my breath. Every time that I'm with this girl is out of this world. It keeps getting better and better.

I ease out to take care of the condom. When I return, Gabi has taken off her heels and is now lying in the bed.

Gabi

This is round three but who's counting. We both know that tonight is our last night together and we're trying to make the most of our time together.

I begin riding Jake. I'm taking it slow because I'm a little sore, but I'm not leaving without getting my fill.

I look down to see Jake looking at me with a sexy intensity that sends a shiver down my spine.

"Take what you want, Gabi."

"Help me, Jake. I'm running out of steam, but this feels amazing."

He takes my hips in his hands, begins pumping me up and down. He's setting the perfect pace. I can tell that I'm about to have another orgasm. I've lost count what number this is at this point. I take my hand and begin playing with my clit.

I close my eyes and enjoy Jake. He's stroking me good. We're working together to bring each other pleasure. Thank god for being in sync. I'm having an out of body experience. I'm about to come so I don't hold back.

"Ah, ah, ah, I'm coming, I'm coming. Oh, god, this is good, so good, Jake."

I continue to ride Jake while purposely contracting around him. I can tell that he likes it because he starts lifting me up and down harder. The muscles in his forearm are bulging, and by the look on his face, he's close.

"Shit, shit, baby, you feel so damn good, so damn good," Jake continues to chant.

He holds me down as his orgasm takes over.

Once he's done, I fall forward, out of breath. We've worked up a sweat but I'm so sated that I'm not sure how much longer that I'll be able to keep my eyes open.

Jake kisses my temple and whispers in my ear, "I'll be right back, baby."

I'm falling asleep when I feel Jake pull me into his arms while kissing the back of my head.

Chapter 10

Jake

    I wake to find I'm alone. I should be mad, but I know that she needs to prepare to disembark. Last night and early morning were amazing. Just thinking about it and I'm hard. We'd still be in bed if I had my way.

As I'm packing up my toiletry bag, I hear a text come in. I pick up my phone and see that it's Gabi.

Gabi: Thank you for an amazing night and making this cruise my best vacation ever. It was nice meeting you.

I have to read her text several times and each time I'm experiencing a range of emotions from hurt to anger. I'm fuming as I walk to Gabi's suite. I knock harder than I probably should, but I am having a difficult time reining in my anger?

"WHAT THE FUCK is this!"

I can tell that Gabi is surprised that I'm angry with the text by the look on her face.

"I thought that it was best to let you know how much fun that I had with you," says Gabi in a pragmatic way.

"WHAT DO YOU MEAN BY SENDING ME THIS TEXT? Really, Gabi – I heard my phone ding, saw it was you, and thought it was anything but 'Thanks, it's been real. Have a nice life!' Have I ever treated you like this is just a cruise fling? Tell me, have I?"

Gabi

"Jake, I don't know what to think. We've been in our own little bubble all week."

He doesn't understand what it's like to be me. Jake is everything that I've always wanted but have been afraid to dream. If you don't dream, you don't have to worry about being disappointed. The strategy has worked for me – up until this point. I can't allow myself to even think that being in a real relationship with Jake is a possibility because if I take a shot and this doesn't work out, I know that I'll be crushed. No, I'd be heartbroken and maybe not ever recover.

I don't realize that I'm shaking and crying until Jake pulls me into his arms. Once he does, I start to do the ugly cry. I should be embarrassed but I'm beyond caring – he doesn't realize it but he pushed me to my breaking point. I've been trying to keep my feelings at bay and not allow myself to hope that this is real. When I say I'm catching feelings that's an understatement. I'm head over heels in love with this guy. Uhhh – how did I let this happen, and in seven freaking days? The very thing that I didn't want to happen has happened.

Jake

"Shhhh, baby don't cry. I can't stand to see you cry. I'd kick the guy's ass who made you cry, but it appears that guy is me." Seeing her cry breaks my heart. I begin to calm down while I hold her.

She laughs. That's what I wanted to hear. I continue to hold her and let her get it all out. I've thought all week that there's something more going on with her but she hasn't wanted to open up so I've given her the space that she needs. She finally stops crying – I pull her away so she can see my face.

"I'm saying this to you because I want to make sure that you hear me loud and clear. You are more than a fling to me. I want to see you once we're both back home. I know we have to deal with the distance issue, but it's not a deal-breaker for me. So, Gabi, what do you say? I come to Austin all the time and want to keep seeing you. We could climb Mt. Bonnell, canoe on Town Lake, ride bikes, or anything really. I just want to spend more time with you,"

Gabi

My, oh, my – everything on that list is physical. What if I'm unable to do some of the activities? I've been tired off and on during this week, but I'm not sure if it was more to do with me only getting four to five hours of a sleep a night for the past three weeks leading up to the cruise due to the project that I'm on or something else. I've enjoyed this week where I could escape reality but I have to return to the real world and have my first round of tests when I get back. I hate not telling Jake but now is not the time. I'll find a way to tell him what's going on when we see each other next week.

Gabi – you have not answered the man, and he's staring at you with so much – so much what – they say that your eyes are the window to your soul – I swear that I see hope, anticipation, and something else, it's right there but I can't put my finger on it – ok, stop trying to find an excuse and get it together, girl.

"Jake, I would love spending more time with you and everything that you've mentioned sounds great, especially this time of year before it gets too hot."

"Great, great – how about next weekend? I'd love to spend the day with you. I was thinking that we could have breakfast at Kirby Lane, maybe lunch at Chuy's downtown and see the sunset at The Oasis for dinner. We can fill in the time in between with whatever you like."

I can think of several things that I'd like to do with Jake but I'll try to think really hard to find some PG rated things to do.

"Love it – it's a date. You know I had a wonderful time, Jake – don't you?"

"It was my pleasure. I needed this cruise something fierce. Last year was a horrible year – it's been nice to unplug – meeting you is truly the icing on the cake, but I'm more excited about continuing to see you after the cruise."

Jake grabs me and kisses me like he's trying to tell me everything he can't say. Like I'm something special to him and he never wants to let me go. I get out of my head and just enjoy it. This man is funny, thoughtful, loyal according to his friend, and a brainiac like me. If I didn't know better, I'd say that he's my perfect match. I guess time will tell on whether we can build upon what we started on the cruise. I wonder...could this be love?

To Be Continued...

Want more Gabi and Jake? Read Part II in *For You to Love*

Books by CD Giles

A Love Blossoms Series Novel
Could This Be Love, Book #1

For You to Love, Book #2

Next Book in Series
Jacqui and Travis, Book #3

Don't miss out!

Visit the website below and you can sign up to receive emails whenever CD Giles publishes a new book. There's no charge and no obligation.

https://books2read.com/r/B-A-BNJU-JWGAC

BOOKS 2 READ

Connecting independent readers to independent writers.

About the Author

Living in the Texas Hill Country with her husband of nearly twenty years, CD Giles is a romantic at heart. Her storybook reunion with her sweetheart began in junior high school. After twenty-two years of bad timing and missed opportunities, the stars finally aligned during a group trip together as adults. They've been together ever since their official first date. C.D. loves a good happily-ever-after story--after all, she's living one! When she's not penning one herself, she's watching rom-coms and spending time with family.

    Website: www.cdgiles.com
    Instagram: https://instagram.com/cdgilesauthor/
    Read more at https://cdgiles.com/.